Physics. E   KR   Q   Vol QK

B80

cottan cop

griffin   P Haswell
                        E9

TM

D0861659

SPECIAL MESSAGE TO READERS

This book is published under the auspices of

THE ULVERSCROFT FOUNDATION

(registered charity No. 264873 UK)

Established in 1972 to provide funds for research, diagnosis and treatment of eye diseases. Examples of contributions made are: —

A Children's Assessment Unit at
Moorfield's Hospital, London.

•

Twin operating theatres at the
Western Ophthalmic Hospital, London.

•

A Chair of Ophthalmology at the
Royal Australian College of Ophthalmologists.

•

The Ulverscroft Children's Eye Unit at the
Great Ormond Street Hospital For Sick Children,
London.

You can help further the work of the Foundation by making a donation or leaving a legacy. Every contribution, no matter how small, is received with gratitude. Please write for details to:

THE ULVERSCROFT FOUNDATION,
The Green, Bradgate Road, Anstey,
Leicester LE7 7FU, England.
Telephone: (0116) 236 4325

In Australia write to:
THE ULVERSCROFT FOUNDATION,
c/o The Royal Australian and New Zealand
College of Ophthalmologists,
94-98 Chalmers Street, Surry Hills,

SHOOT-OUT AT BIG KING

Billy Bandro arrives in Freshwater Creek in Wyoming to start a new life away from riding with the killer outlaw Wesley Toms. When Toms is captured, Billy is assigned to drive him to Laramie for trial, but Toms' gang bushwhack the coach, leave Billy for dead, and take Nancy Partridge and her Aunt Emily hostage. The gambler Slam Beardsley saves Billy, and they ride off in pursuit. But there are many surprises for them in the mountains . . .

LEE LEJEUNE

SHOOT-OUT
AT
BIG KING

Complete and Unabridged

LINFORD
Leicester

K 2

First published in Great Britain in 2007 by
Robert Hale Limited
London

First Linford Edition
published 2008
by arrangement with
Robert Hale Limited
London

The moral right of the author has been asserted

Copyright © 2007 by Lee Lejeune
All rights reserved

British Library CIP Data

Lejeune, Lee
    Shoot-out at Big King.—Large print ed.—
Linford western library
    1. Western stories
    2. Large type books
    I. Title
    823.9′2 [F]

    ISBN 978–1–84782–355–7

Published by
F. A. Thorpe (Publishing)
Anstey, Leicestershire

Set by Words & Graphics Ltd.
Anstey, Leicestershire
Printed and bound in Great Britain by
T. J. International Ltd., Padstow, Cornwall

This book is printed on acid-free paper

1

When Billy Bandro drifted into Freshwater Creek, the Reverend Jim Mullins said with his usual gallows humour, 'Looks like a big black crow taking refuge from a cinder storm. Like he's been riding from the pit of hell since the dawn of time.'

The mayor shifted his plug of tobacco from one side of his jaw to the other and ruminated. 'Got a ramrod back though and packs a shooter in a way suggests he could use it.'

'Could have an unhealthy past,' the Reverend Mullins speculated morbidly.

'Guess he might have,' the mayor agreed. 'You never know with drifters. From a distance, his face looks like it was carved out of rock.'

'But close to he seems amiable enough,' the reverend said.

'Doesn't talk much, I hear,' said the

1

mayor. 'But speaks friendly enough when he does.'

Billy was amiable in his approach to the 800 or so citizens in Freshwater Creek. Amiable but guarded. Nobody knew about his past or his future and nobody liked to ask. He got a job in the store and, when things were quiet, which was often the case, he rode shotgun on the Walker stage that went through to Laramie. Everyone learned he was good with a gun because six months later a bunch of hooded riders had attempted a stagecoach hold-up in the wooded country between Freshwater and Red Rock Station and Billy had seen them off decisively with his Winchester '73, killing two clean as shooting salmon in a river. So decisive that old Jake Jacks, the tobacco-chewing stage driver, a man of wide experience and acknowledged wisdom, had spat a whole stream of tobacco juice into the dust and raised his voice in praise.

'Ain't hardly never seen such impressive shootin',' he .declared. 'Those nincompoop raiders hightailed it just like they had the flames of hell up their arses.'

So Billy had acquired a reputation as a man who was safe to ride with and that made him permanent on the stage.

He was sitting in the Bronco Saloon early on the evening when Marshal Eldridge Leaver brought in Wesley Toms, when a boy crept in like a cautious mouse and bowed down like a page in the palace of a king.

'Excuse me, Mr Bandro, sir. You're wanted down at the depot.'

Billy was hauling in a well-earned pint. Most of the day he'd been hefting huge packages around in the store, so he was thirsty.

'Who wants me, boy?' he grinned. As the mayor had said, he had one of those faces that seem blank and unfriendly till they smile. For the boy it was like the sun bursting over the distant mountains.

'It's Mr Gus Felixstowe, sir. He says he wants to speak with you right away,

3

if that's OK, sir.'

'Right away, is it?' Billy reached into his vest pocket and flipped a dime on to the table. 'Tell Mr Gus Felixstowe I'll be down just as soon as I've refreshed myself with this swill. And buy yourself a candy bar. Looks like you need it with all this rushing around and bowing down you're doing.'

The kid slapped his hand on the dime and reeled it in. 'Thank you, sir. I'll do it right away, sir.'

'And another thing,' Billy said. 'Don't do so much scraping the floor with your knees. That way you're liable to get splinters. And cut out a few of those 'sirs' you keep throwing around in case folks get the idea you're rehearsing for the part of page boy in one of those fancy theatre productions they do back, East.'

'Yes, sir. Thank you, sir.' The boy made a grovelling motion with his hands, stuck the dime in the pocket of his pants, and backed away, dumbfounded by all this high-flown talk from

4

a man who generally had hardly a word to say.

Billy finished his beer at his leisure and wiped his mouth with the back of his hand.

'Did you see those mighty fine folks in town?' John Steegles crowed from behind the bar.

'I didn't see no fine folk. Thought they all stayed east of the Mississippi,' Billy said. 'Who would these turkeys be anyway, Johnny?'

'Just got in from way back East as you said, Billy. Two fine ladies in city duds and some sort of fancy gambler with rings as big as knucklebones on his fingers. On their way to Laramie, pulling out on tomorrow's stage, I hear.'

'That so?' Billy got up from the table and adjusted his belt. His eyes twinkled with amusement as he addressed the barman. 'Two fine city ladies, you say?'

'Sure thing, Billy.' Steegles licked his lips. 'One of them sort of old and homey with a lot of mouth. Can't stop yapping all the time. The other one young and tender and a joy to the eye. Staying at the Grand tonight, though what's grand about it I wouldn't like to speculate.'

Billy approached the bar, took a coin from his pants pocket and spun it The barman watched it with a fascinated grin and slapped a hand on it like he thought it might try to escape when it stopped spinning on the bar. 'You wouldn't know grand if they shoved it right up your left nostril,' Billy told him.

The barman snorted and swung a fake punch at the younger man.

★ ★ ★

Gus Felixstowe, the manager of the Walker Stage Company, was sitting behind his desk trying to look more important than he was. A Humpty Dumpty sort of man with an egg-like head and side whiskers that must have tickled his wife silly when they made love, which was probably none too frequent. Maybe whiskers is all he has, Billy speculated.

'Ah, Billy,' Felixstowe said, removing a ten-cent cigar from his chops, and blowing out a highly inflated puff of blue smoke. 'Tomorrow we got an important assignment for you.'

Billy nodded twice and said nothing.

'I guess you heard about the arrest of Toms?'

'I did hear something,' Billy said, noncommitally. He knew that Marshal Eldridge Leaver had brought in the bank robber and murderer Wesley Toms earlier the day before and banged him up in the town calaboose.

Felixstowe shot him a self-important look. 'What d'you know about Toms, Billy?'

Billy's grey-blue eyes narrowed. 'What should I know about Toms?'

Felixstowe cleared his throat nervously. 'I never said you should know nothing, Billy. It's just that I hear rumours. Sitting behind this desk the whole world floats in and lands in front of you. Even some things that ain't strictly true.'

Billy met his eye directly. 'So what did you hear this time?'

Felixstowe shrugged his fat shoulders. 'I didn't say I heard anything in particular. I just heard rumours you and Toms had crossed trails together one time.'

Billy considered for a moment. Everyone in Freshwater Creek knew about Toms and his associates. They had been a wart on the backside of Northern Colorado and Wyoming for the past fifteen years: thieving, robbing banks, holding up stages, etc.

'Who's spreading these rumours?' he asked.

'Well, now,' Felixstowe said defensively, 'nobody in particular. The preacher says you came from Colorado. You know how the Reverend Jim Mullins likes to throw rumours around like they're plugs of tobacco.'

'Mullins likes to talk,' Billy agreed.

'More like it would be the sheriff,' he suggested.

Felixstowe nodded. 'Could be Sheriff Watts. He has to keep his ear close to the ground. That's part of his job.'

Billy's eyes narrowed again. 'Watts has a poisonous tongue like an old widow woman I once knew. You suggesting you got doubts about me, Mr Felixstowe?'

Felixstowe held up a pudgy hand. 'Now, I never said that, Billy. You've done a good job with this stage line 'specially when you drove off those stage hold-up men that time, and I'm not the man to forget that.' He leaned forward across his desk intently. 'If you tell me you never met Toms, why, that's good enough for me.'

Billy shook his head slowly. He prided himself on one thing in particular: he was a straight shootist in word and gun. 'I didn't say we never met. We did meet one time,' he replied acidly. 'I knew Toms long enough to find out he was a rattlesnake in the form of a man

9

if that's any help to you.'

Felixstowe considered for a moment and shook his head. 'We have to ask these questions, Billy. I'm sure you know that. Toms is an ace prisoner. It's important we get him through to Laramie nice and easy so they can hang him.'

Billy grinned. 'Ain't that Marshal Leaver's business?' He knew Marshal Leaver had brought in Toms the night before but didn't know how Toms had been caught. Could have been a tip off, he thought. You don't catch men like Toms easy.

Gus Felixstowe stuck his ten-cent cigar between his lips and ruminated for half a minute. Billy looked up at the ceiling and waited, remembering the time ten years back when he had met Toms down in Colorado: a criminal with the charm of a hypnotizing rattlesnake in the Garden of Eden.

'Speaks like a politician, shoots like a circus sharp shooter,' Billy summed Toms up. 'Don't know how Leaver got the drop on him without getting himself killed stone dead.'

The manager leaned forward like a hippopotamus with a sore throat. 'I want you to take the small stage to Laramie tomorrow. You'll drive and Marshal Eldridge Leaver and the prisoner will be inside.'

'All the way to Laramie?' Billy said. 'Sounds cosy. Who's riding shotgun?'

Felixstowe nodded. 'There won't be no shotgun, Billy. You'll be your own shotgun. That way you won't attract too much attention.'

Billy ruminated for a moment. 'What about the regular stage?'

Felixstowe nodded again. He had that figured. 'The regular stage will pull out earlier. Jake Jacks will drive. He'll take Miss Emily Partridge and her niece Nancy and the other passengers.'

'Does that include the gambling man they speak of, the one with rings like rocks on his fingers?'

'You see him?' Felixstowe said.

'I heard about him,' Billy said.

11

'He's one of the passengers on the regular stage,' Felixstowe confirmed.

'I hope you instructed old man Jacks to keep off the bottle,' Billy commented, sardonically.

'Jake never let me down yet,' Felixstowe snapped. 'Anyways, I don't have another driver. That's why I'm asking you to drive the second coach which will leave from the back door of the gaol half an hour later. We don't want to attract unwanted attention, do we?'

'I think we already did that,' Billy said. 'In a small two-bit town like this everyone knows what's happening, even when the mayor blows his nose, or the preacher gives an accidental fart. But that's no never mind.'

Felixstowe scribbled something on a pad. 'Marshal Leaver will notify Laramie you're on your way. Needless to say, you'll pack your shooter and the shotgun and that useful Winchester '73 of yourn.'

Billy grinned. 'You don't have to

teach your mouse how to eat cheese, Mr Felixstowe,' he said.

Felixstowe ignored the insult. 'Get your rest, Billy,' he said. 'Remember, there could be a big bonus in this for you.'

'Is that right?' Billy got up from his chair. 'How much would that be, Mr Felixstowe?'

The Manager's face creased in a knowing smile. 'The usual, Billy, the usual . . . plus a little more . . . maybe.'

He placed a finger against his bulbous nose and nodded portentously.

2

Billy was nowhere ready for sleep. He had other things on his mind. He went back to his attic high up in Ma Hungerford's rooming-house where he laid out his artillery on top of yesterday's *Freshwater Star* on the bed: the shotgun, the Winchester '73, and the Remington pistol which he had acquired several years before and for which he had a strange affection.

After checking the weaponry and stocking up the gunbelt with cartridges, he strapped the belt to his waist, eased the holster with the Remington into a snug position, not too low and not too high, against his thigh, and tied the leather thong to his leg.

Then he took a stroll down Main Street, past the Grand hotel, and on to the Bronco Saloon where he usually ate his supper. Everything was quiet, quieter than usual in town, but this didn't reassure Billy. He felt sort of prickly and on edge like there was a spook around every corner waiting to gun him down. Billy wasn't normally a nervous man, but ever since the bushwhacking episode when he had driven off the potential gold thieves and shot two of them to death, he had felt a kind of creepy feeling at the back of his neck. Nobody else saw it and nobody knew, but it made him cautious. You never knew who wanted revenge on you for doing what you thought was right. And, anyway, this business with Toms had a nasty taste to it. Toms had that invincible reputation and you knew he wouldn't let himself be taken in without somebody getting killed.

As he strolled on under the lemon yellow lights from the Grand Hotel he saw a squat grizzly figure in a high hat moving towards him down the street. He recognized it immediately as Sheriff Watts.

'Why, hello there, Billy!' the sheriff

greeted him, in a high, hillbilly kind of voice.

'Evening, Sheriff Watts,' Billy said. 'Why are you walking out so late?' Billy had learned to treat the local lawman coolly but civilly.

Watts was chewing a plug of tobacco. He had a gunbelt slung across his fat belly and looked like a slob who could never reach his gun. But Billy knew Watts could be venomous and he also knew Watts disliked him for some reason. Probably thought he was cocky and superior.

'Just patrolling,' Watts said casually. 'You hear we got Toms under lock and key?' He was staring at Billy warily from under the brim of his black hat.

'I heard,' Billy said. 'Rumour flies fast in this town.'

Watts showed his broken teeth in a grin. 'I have another rumour,' he said.

'What's that then?'

Watts ruminated a moment. 'Some say you rode with Toms down in Colorado some time. Strange how rumour carries on the wind, eh?'

Billy nodded. 'You don't want to believe everything you hear, Sheriff.'

Watts continued to grin. 'Does that mean you did, or you didn't?'

Billy held up his head. He was a good six inches taller than the sheriff. He was thirty years old and when he set his jaw he looked like a totem statue. 'That means I do know Toms and I fell in with him one time when I was too young to know better. Now I do know better and I know Toms is a killer who deserves what he gets.'

Watts nodded and seemed satisfied. 'That's good,' he said, 'because Felixstowe tells me you're the man to drive him up to Laramie so he can get hanged.'

'That's a lot of trouble to go to and a real big risk to take with a killer like Toms. You could give him the drop right here.'

Watts gave a deep growl of a laugh. 'We could do that, but it wouldn't be quite legal like. So you got to deliver him like a parcelled-up turkey for Thanksgiving with Marshal Eldridge Leaver. Is that clear enough?'

'That's clear enough,' Billy said.

'And another thing,' Watts continued, 'it might not be an easy ride. Other rumours have it that Toms has friends and acquaintances, men who owe him a favour or two. So you got to look out for yourself.'

'I know about Toms's friends,' Billy said. Something about the tone of the sheriff's voice increased the bad feeling back of his neck. He guessed that as far as Watts was concerned he was expendable. But Marshal Eldridge Leaver was reliable and straight in Billy's experience. So that made a difference.

'By the way,' Watts said slyly, 'Toms has been asking to see you so I guess he must think he knows you anyway.' His eyes under the brim of the black hat looked cat-like and even more suspicious.

'Is there any reason why I should

want to talk to your prisoner?' Billy asked coolly.

'Not one reason in the world,' the sheriff agreed. 'He says he wants to hand over a gold watch to an old friend, that's all.'

Billy saw the gleam of derision in the sheriff's eye and knew he was being put to some kind of test.

'If Toms wants to give away his gold watch, I suggest he hands it over to the orphanage. That way maybe St Peter will slide open the gate there more easily. Let's hope he isn't as corrupt as Toms is.'

'That's a good answer, Billy,' the sheriff laughed. His laugh was like the creak of a barn door that needed oiling. Watts shrugged his shoulders and moved off in the direction of the sheriff's office and the jail.

Billy stopped to consider under the lemon tinted light from the Grand hotel. He knew Watts had never trusted him and might be trying to put something on him; something to do with the way he had shot up those bushwhackers and killed two of them when they were trying to steal the gold maybe. For some reason he couldn't quite figure, he caught a distinct and ugly picture of Toms in his mind: the man's oily tongue and the blackened teeth under his curling lip.

Suddenly he heard a faint sound, and, looking up, saw a kind of vision in the form of a young woman leaning on the balcony and watching him from above.

His hand went to his Stetson in a brief salute. 'Good evening, ma'am.'

The girl smiled. 'Good evening, sir.' She spoke with gentle irony and made a slight suggestion of a curtsy. The light slanted from a window behind her, caught her in a kind of halo. Possibly she'd seen *Romeo and Juliet* performed back East and recognized the humour in her situation. As if to give point to that irony, a door behind her opened suddenly and an older, somewhat stiff, female figure appeared.

'Come along in, Nancy. We have a long day before us tomorrow. You'll need to get your rest,' the stiff female figure said in a cracked voice.

The girl turned, then half turned back again and briefly raised her hand. 'Goodnight, sir,' she said.

'Good night to you,' Billy said, and the vision disappeared behind lace curtains leaving him kind of breathless.

★   ★   ★

Before climbing the stairs to the upper room in the Bronco Saloon where he usually took his supper, Billy walked along to the sheriff's office and saw outside the sprawling figure of Marshal Eldridge Leaver swinging gently to and fro on a rocking chair with a Winchester across his knees.

'Hi there, Billy!' Eldridge raised his hand and Billy perched himself on a bench beside him.

'Did Felixstowe tell you I'm your driver for tomorrow?' Billy said.

'I told him,' the marshal said stoutly. 'I insisted on it, Billy. This is a big assignment. I wanted a man who is good with a gun who I could trust.'

Billy nodded. 'I take that as a compliment. How come you took Toms so easy?' he said.

'Not so easy,' Leaver objected. 'I got the drop on him through a jealous woman.'

'That so?' Billy's lip curled sardonically.

Leaver shrugged his muscular shoulders. 'Never trust an old lover,' he said. 'I got word Toms was lying drunk as a dog in a ranch house I don't choose to name. So I walked in nice and easy and got a gun on him. Tied him up tight as a turkey before he could hardly wake, and brought him into town. Easiest arrest I made since they pinned on my marshal's shield.'

'Sounds good and easy. But why don't they send a posse up from Laramie to take Toms in?'

Eldridge Leaver frowned. 'That would

be a good idea, Billy, but we don't have the time or the reliable men. I telegraphed Laramie to send an escort but they're tied up dealing with something big up there. And Sheriff Watts has things to do here. We keep Toms in the jail here long enough someone would sure enough try to spring him. So it's up to you and me.'

'So you think he'd be safer on the road?' Billy asked dubiously.

Leaver paused to consider. 'It's a matter of judgement.' He glanced sideways at Billy. 'I know some people in this here town don't trust you, Billy, but I know you better than they do.'

'Then I guess that's enough for me.'

Under the shade of the overhang the two men reached out and shook hands.

* * *

Billy walked into the sheriff's office and saw Sheriff Watts whittling a hickory stick at the official table, a six-shooter handy on the desk in front of him.

'Hello, Billy! So we meet again,' the sheriff greeted. 'You decided to look in and see Toms after all then. You got your official pass?' He gave a low sardonic chuckle.

'Just thought I'd check in like you said, see the prisoner had his goodnight toddy,' Billy said.

He peered between the bars of the cell in which Wesley Toms seemed to be sleeping with his black Stetson pulled down close over his eyes and one knee crooked high on the bunk. Despite the half-hidden face Billy recognized the close-shaved lean jawbone. Whatever Toms might be, he always turned himself out well. Took a shave every morning except in the most desperate circumstances and changed his shirt at least once every two weeks. Billy remembered the old times when he had fallen in with the Toms outfit when it had seemed the sort of high bravado a young man should enjoy — a yardstick against which he could measure his manhood. But Toms had soon shown his dark side and Billy knew he was a dangerous and ruthless killer — a man who would stop at nothing against those who stood in his way. It was a good thing they were taking him to be hanged.

As he looked down at the apparently sleeping form, the lips under the brim of the Stetson grinned slowly. Billy caught a glimpse of the vicious gold tooth under the curling lip and the long remembered voice of the outlaw came out clear and strong. 'Hi there, Billy boy. How you doin'? I didn't know you'd taken to the law so hard. Recognized your voice soon as I heard you talking to the marshal out there.'

Billy said nothing and, after a moment, the outlaw flipped back his Stetson and swung forward to sit on the bunk. Even behind bars, he looked ready and willing to pull a gun and blast a man to Kingdom Come.

'You come to spring me out of the hoosegow or something?'

Billy gave Toms a tight grin. 'No such

luck, Wesley. I'm afraid your doomsday bell has started to toll. I believe you have an appointment with the judge and the hangman in Laramie.'

Toms gave a low snigger. 'Sounds like you lost your guts, Billy Boy. I always knew you had a delicate stomach. Remember this.' He wagged a finger at the bars separating him from Billy. 'We ain't in Laramie yet. Could be the powers above have other plans for Mr Toms. You hear me, boy? I always was a religious man, you know that.'

'I hear you, Mr Toms. I hear you bragging just like in the old days when you thought you were halfway to Washington.'

Toms sniggered again darkly. He leaned forward like a tiger at the bars. 'Don't push your luck, boy,' he snarled. Then his voice softened and he smiled. 'You don't happen to have the makings for a quirly you could spare, do you? I could sure use a smoke. Or a big turkey dinner. Or a bottle of rye for that matter. How about a drink for old time's sake?'

Billy looked at the hairs glistening on the backs of the knuckles clutching the bars and shook his head. 'I don't think so, Toms. From now on you have to get used to gaol chow with water.'

'That is till they hang you,' Sheriff Watts put in from behind the table.

Toms shook his head. 'You could be right, Sheriff. And there again you could be wrong.' His eyes fixed on Billy again. 'I see you've grown in respectability, Billy, since we last met. So why don't we just shake hands for ol' time's sake? And, by the way, I have a watch I want to give you. Real full-carat gold. Got it from an old miner friend down in Colorado. Wanted me to have it in memory of our deep friendship for one another.'

'After you shot him, you mean?' Billy said laconically.

Toms laughed. 'You're a hard critter, Billy, but you still have a sense of humour.'

'Keep the watch,' Billy said. 'Give it to the gallows man so he drops you clean and fast.'

Toms laughed again. 'That's really considerate of you, Billy. And I'll hand him your respects with it so he remembers you when your time comes. Let's shake on it.'

The thought of taking Toms's hand made Billy stiffen and he gave a low sceptical chuckle. 'Thanks for the offer. Mr Toms. I think I'll pass on that one.'

'You're no sucker,' Toms laughed. 'See you tomorrow, dude.'

Billy nodded to the sheriff and went to the door. Marshal Leaver was still on the rocking chair on the porch with the Winchester across his knees.

'Still the same high-horse bastard,' the marshal remarked.

Billy stopped and turned. 'Keep out of the light, Eldridge. You might have taken Toms easy when he was drunk. But remember, he has friends and associates, and it only takes one shot to kill a man.'

3

As Billy walked along Main Street to the Bronco Saloon, he heard the noise of merrymaking: hoots of laughter and snatches of the 'Old Colonial Boy'. But the sounds gave him no comfort; instead, they increased his sense of impending trouble. Seeing Toms again had made his stomach crawl like he had just eaten something he would later throw up. He remembered the old days when Toms had left him to guard the horses while he and his bunch sneaked up to break into a bank some place across the border. Worse, he remembered when Toms had shot a man in cold blood for shouting obscenities at him. That was when Billy had broken away and decided to mend his life. He knew that Toms deserved all he got from the law, but, in spite of his hard words about the hangman, he still had mixed feelings about Toms, who seemed so bright and amiable — the man who had befriended him in Colorado.

As he approached the saloon, he checked the horses at the hitching rail and saw there were several he hadn't seen before: a big bay with a fancy saddle, for instance. When he pushed his way in through the swing doors, he noticed two things immediately: the bunch of men around the old strung-out piano where Lou Lou held court. Lou Lou was regarded as a fancy woman of the town, but she had a generous heart and could coax a rousing melody from even the most clapped out joanna. She could dance, too, when Stan Bird's Eye struck the chords, and sometimes she sang like a bird though her voice had the husky tone of a kid that cried itself to sleep at night.

The other thing he noticed in particular was the big crowd gathered around the card table where a marathon poker game was in progress. The game included at least two new faces: an older guy with rings like knuckle bones on his fingers, and a younger, bearded *hombre* wearing a tooled vest. The guy in the tooled vest had a face like a Navajo mask, sickly green in the reflection from the baize surface of the table. He must be the one riding the big bay with the fancy saddle. The other man, the one in the dark suit with the knuckle-size rings, had fingers that riffled through the cards like water rippling down the rapids. Billy figured on him being the one who had checked in from the stage that afternoon.

'Hi, Billy,' the barman John Steegles crowed. 'We got us a busy night here, man.'

'You sure do,' Billy said.

Steegles winked across the bar. 'I'll send word up to do your steak just the way you like it. We don't want to upset our regular customers, do we now?'

'That's the way to keep them happy.' Billy touched his nose. 'I see you got a big game on over there.' He jerked his thumb towards the poker game that was attracting so much attention.

Steegles wagged his head to and fro. 'That gambling man who blew in on the stage this afternoon is a wizard with the cards. He shuffles so quick it's a blur. He's going on the stage to Laramie tomorrow morning after he's cleaned us out here, he and those two ladies I mentioned. The old crab and and the young peach.'

Billy grinned. 'Yeah. I caught a glimpse of the two ladies you mentioned up at the Grand earlier.'

'That so?' Steegles laughed. 'Don't get above your station, boy. They tell me those two ladies are associated with a big spread down Laramie way. The girl's father is one of the swellest ranchers in the region.'

'Is that right?' Billy leaned his elbows on the bar. 'And who's that guy with the fancy waistcoat and a face like an Injun statue with whiskers?'

Steegles glanced at the gambling table just as the man they were referring to looked up and fixed his gaze in their direction. 'I don't know who he is,' Steegles said in a low voice, as though the man could hear them. 'But seems like he has mystical powers, or the ears of a coyote, from the way he's looking across at us. Rode in late this afternoon. Did you see his fancy saddle?'

'I saw it. I wonder why he hasn't taken it off to give his horse a rest. Probably wants to impress us country folk.' He tossed his head. 'I guess I'll go up for my chow.'

Billy took note of the wooden-faced *hombre* as he mounted the stairs to the dining area where he usually took his supper. As he put his hand on the bannister rail, Lou Lou stopped thumping the keyboard amidst a round of applause. 'Hello, Billy,' she called. 'Are you dining with us tonight?'

'Going up right now.'

'Mind if I join you for a drink?'

'That'll be my pleasure, Lou Lou.'

He sat in his usual corner with his

back to the wall. Though he had no reason to be suspicious, he always sat that way because he knew of many foolish or foolhardy dandies like William Butler Hickock who had been gunned down from behind while they were in the middle of a poker game or a well-cooked supper.

Before his steak arrived, Lou Lou slid into the chair opposite and beamed across at him. Her face was a mask, of course: overdone mascara, heavy lines, and exaggerated lips. But it was all part of the trade and Billy knew that underneath all the grease and paint there was the face of a kind and beautiful woman. He had often wondered what had brought such a lovely woman into the bar-room trade.

'The boys are enjoying themselves tonight,' he said, pouring her a drink of rye.

'Fantasy,' she said. 'I feed their dreams, you know.'

'Sure,' he said as the steak arrived. 'You want to eat with me, Lou Lou?'

'You're one sweet man, Billy.' The mask cracked again and Billy could see little rivulets of perspiration trickling through the powder. 'I don't eat while I'm on duty, you know. I just play and sing. Stan will be playing soon and they'll expect me to dance.'

Billy took a mouthful and began to chew. 'I want to tell you something, Lou. You're worth a whole lot better than playing and dancing for bums in an outfit like this. Did anyone ever tell you that?'

She raised her glass and looked at him steadily from behind it. 'You know, Billy, that's the nicest thing you said to me.'

'Well, it's true, you know,' he mumbled. 'I've been meaning to tell you that since I first started eating my suppers up here.'

She gave him a tinkling laugh. 'I could be persuaded to take a trip to the moon with someone like you, you know.' She took a sip of booze. 'Anyway, Billy, I could say the same thing to you. A man of your talent riding shotgun on a rattle-bone stage when he should be doing something a whole lot more worthwhile.' Her voice rang with deep sincerity.

'Like what for instance?' he asked.

'Well now, Billy.' She closed her eyes. 'You could be a newspaper editor, or even a great writer. Did you ever think of that?'

Billy paused with a morsel of steak hovering close to his mouth. 'A great writer! You must be kidding! I couldn't even write a letter to my grandmother.'

'I really think you could, Billy,' she said. 'You have a good way with words, you know.'

'Words don't count for much in a town like this.' All the same it made him think: maybe he could be doing something a lot more worthwhile.

A bell sounded somewhere below.

She drank back her rye and rose abruptly. 'I got to go now, Billy. Stan Bird's Eye's here. They'll want me to dance.'

She turned and hesitated, and then turned back. 'I don't know what's happening tomorrow, Billy, but I hear rumours. And I want you to promise me something.'

'What's that?' he asked.

'You take care now,' she said.

Before he could reply she had blown him a kiss and run towards the stairs.

As he settled down to eat the rest of his steak he thought of the nice things she had said. Then his mind turned to Toms again. He knew that Toms would kill him and anyone else who got in his way if he had a chance. A man who is on his way to hang doesn't have too much conscience about taking a few more with him.

4

On his way down the stairs, Billy saw the man with the Injun-mask face turn and stare at him again as though marking him down for a future encounter. The wooden face looked familiar, though Billy couldn't remember him from the past. The gambler with the knuckle rings was raking in his winnings and the poker game seemed about to break up with grumblings and rumblings from some of the other players who had lost heavily during the evening. Lou Lou was doing her dance routine beside the piano as Stan Bird's Eye bent over the keys in his new-fangled bowler hat and pounded away with a mixture of gusto, showmanship, and sensuality.

As Lou Lou kicked up her legs by the jangly piano, cheers of acclamation rang out and one or two of the old-timers reached out with their grimy fingers and tried to paw at her legs. But Lou Lou beat them off so hard with her fan that they curled up, hugging their knuckles. Billy felt more than a twinge of jealousy. When a roaming cowboy reached up and attempted to grab her by the waist and swing her round, she tried to wriggle free and bat him off, but the roaming cowboy wouldn't stop grabbing at her and pulling her round the floor.

'Come on, baby, treat me nice,' he said. Billy saw that he was young and green and on the way to being roaring drunk.

'You behave nice and someone else will treat you nice,' Lou Lou protested, as she attempted to wriggle out his grasp.

'Oh, come on, babe!' the cowboy persisted, clawing at her breast.

'Why you crawling sidewinder!' Lou Lou drew back her fist and landed the cowboy a handful of knuckles. The cowboy staggered back and half fell.

But he was a mean one in his drink and he came in with a roar like a railroad train on the loose. He might have crushed her against the piano like an injured butterfly, but Billy reached out and grabbed him by his leather vest and held him back.

'Easy there, cowboy!'

The cowboy glared at Billy close to and almost spat on his shirt. 'What's it to you, lover man?'

They were eyeball to red-rimmed eyeball. The wreak of stale whiskey breath assaulted Billy's nostrils.

'Keep your hands to yourself!' he warned.

'Get your paws off'n me!' the cowboy snarled. 'Or I'll pound you right into the ground!'

His face was lean and ugly and his muscles were as tight and as well strung as Bird's Eye's piano. Billy sensed he knew how to hit and to hit hard.

He jerked the cowboy away from Lou Lou and hurled him across the room. Everything in the Bronco Saloon became still and expectant. Heads bobbed up from the pool table and the men around the piano drew back silently waiting for the crash to come.

The cowboy collided with a table and knocked an old-timer on to his back. Then he bounced back with his fists ready to fly every whichway. As he came in roaring, Billy dodged aside and stuck out his foot. The cowboy careered on, falling heavily against the piano and pressing Stan Bird's Eye against the keyboard with a jangling crash of chords.

Before the cowboy could recover and come in again, Billy seized hold of his vest again, spun him round and kicked him right in the middle of his lean rump. The cowboy staggered forward and crashed into another table, upsetting drinks and men in every direction. There was a universal roar of laughter and a deal of cursing from drinkers trying to sponge the booze off their clothes. Yet still the cowboy refused to go down. Roaring, he whirled round

41

snarling like a mountain lion and striking like lightning for the gun on his hip.

Billy was lean, something over six feet tall, and his muscles were taut as tempered steel. Before the cowboy could draw his shooter, his foot had shot out and struck him clean on the jaw. The drunken cowboy reeled back and tumbled hard against the saloon floor.

A considerable gasp went up from the men surrounding Lou Lou at the piano, and they drew back even further to avoid any stray slugs that might come from the enraged cowboy's shooter. But Billy wasn't taking chances. Before the cowboy could recover himself and go for his gun again, Billy seized him by the shoulders and lifted him clean off the floor like a struggling papoose.

He marched the winded cowboy through the swing doors and hurled him with the force of thunder across the broadwalk and on to the dust of the street. Before the cowboy could struggle back on to his feet, Billy drew his Remington and levelled it at his head. 'Don't get any ideas, cowboy,' he said, 'and don't come back till you learn some respect for a lady.'

He stayed with the Remington cocked as the wild-eyed cowboy struggled to his feet.

'You gonna regret that!' the cowboy shouted hoarsely. 'You better watch yourself from now on. You ain't gonna ferget that, mister!'

He limped away into the darkness to lick his injured pride. When Billy could see him no more, he uncocked his pistol and slid it into its holster.

When he went back into the saloon a cheer went up from the crowd, but for some reason Lou Lou had disappeared up the stairs.

'Come and take a drink and cool off,' Johnny Steegles shouted from behind the bar. 'You deserve one on the house for that!'

Billy went to the bar and received several hard thumps on the back, but he felt far from pleased. 'What's with Lou Lou?' he muttered between his teeth.

'Lou Lou's OK.' Steegles laughed. 'You can never tell with a woman, Billy. They're tricky critters, you know.'

He gave a thumbs up to Stan Bird's Eye who had retrieved his newfangled bowler hat. He tipped it back, adjusted his armbands, and struck a familiar chord on the piano. That cooled everyone and initiated a chorus of singing, some of it sharp and some of it distinctly flat and out of tune.

When Billy finished his drink and turned from the bar, he almost bumped into the gambler with the knucklebone rings, who was standing close beside him.

'That was cool piece of work,' the man said in a voice full of gravel. 'I thought you dealt with that rowdy character with something close to finesse.'

Billy nodded ironically. 'Thank you, sir. I appreciate the word of praise.'

'No, really,' the gambler insisted, 'I

mean it. He was asking to be shot and most men would have done it. It would have been self-defence. I admire a man who knows what he wants and goes for the jugular.'

'Nice of you to say so . . . ' Billy said. Now his pulse was beginning to slow he could see both the humour and the danger in the situation and he knew from experience that the drunken cowboy would have put a bullet through his gut if he could have reached his shooter in time.

The gambler stuck out his ring-cluttered fingers. 'I'm Slam Beardsley. I'm a gambling man. I just raked in my winnings.' He grinned with malicious humour. 'I'm leaving on the coach for Laramie tomorrow morning. I under-stand from what I hear you might be keeping us company.'

Billy's eyes narrowed. 'Who told you that, mister?'

'It seems to be the general consensus of opinion. I'm led to believe you ride shotgun on that particular coach most of the time. Is that so?'

The way the man fished around made Billy suspicious. He glanced over at the poker table and saw that the other stranger — the man with the hickory face — had disappeared. 'Sometimes I ride shotgun,' he said. 'Sometimes I just ride. What I'm doing tomorrow is between me and the Walker Company, mister.'

Instead of looking offended, the gambler laughed and nodded. 'No offence. A wise answer, young man. You have a good head on your shoulders. I see that. Take a drink with me. I'm sure you could use a shot of rye.'

Billy didn't often drink with strangers, but on this occasion he relented. They sat at a little round table facing the swing doors. As usual Billy made sure he had his back to the wall, and he noticed Slam Beardsley laughed as he did the same. As the gambler took his seat, he pushed back his long black coat to reveal a studded holster and a handy Smith & Wesson .38.

'You been in this town long?' Slam Beardsley enquired.

'Long enough to learn,' Billy said.

'You seem to have earned some respect.' The gambler gave him a long look from under his droopy eyebrows. 'A man of your ability should have ambitions. You know that?'

'I have my ambitions,' Billy countered.

The gambler twirled his fingers through his long, wispy moustache. 'Could be,' he said, 'I might put you in the way of improving your position in life. That is if you had a mind to it.'

'Sounds interesting,' Billy said with slight irony. 'But first maybe you could fill me in on that hard-faced *hombre* sitting in on the card game with you half an hour back.'

A cunning gleam darted in Slam Beardsley's flinty eyes. 'That's a very interesting question,' he said. ''cause he was asking me the same about you, like you were a long-lost brother or something. You sure you haven't seen him before?'

47

That was an interesting question. Billy was almost sure. You don't forget a face that looks as though it's been carved out of a hickory post.

Then suddenly a light shone out in his head and the word 'Colorado' started flashing! Jeremiah Dandy, he thought. It could be Jeremiah Dandy! Jeremiah Dandy was a hard son-of-a-bitch. Reputation as a marksman. Could be he had ridden with Wesley Toms some time. Maybe he still was. Billy couldn't be sure, but he knew one thing: Jeremiah Dandy spelt danger!

5

Come sun-up Billy was standing in the doorway of the Walker Stage Company office watching the hands load up the stage to Laramie. Out on the sidewalk, the Humpty Dumpty figure of Gus Felixstowe, the manager, with his thumbs twanging his suspenders, shouted orders to the loaders in his high, prairie-chicken voice. The loaders ignored him as they heaved the valises and cases into the loading bay at the rear of the coach, and old Jake, the coach driver greeted the passengers with bows that were as extravagant and formal as his arthritic body would permit. Billy had seen him drinking heavily in the Bronco Saloon the night before and Jake had been one of those who had cheered most loudly when Billy floored the cowboy and booted him out of the saloon. But hard drinking was nothing new for old Jake who was such an accomplished imbiber he could easily drink anyone in Freshwater under the table and walk away as sober as Socrates.

In the morning sunshine, Billy saw the passengers arriving: a middle-aged bank employee, a salesman in a thread-bare flannel suit, and Slam Beardsley, the gambler. Beardsley looked around, saw Billy standing in the doorway, and gave a wry grin as though he guessed he'd been wrong about Billy riding shotgun and knew the reason why. In fact, there was no shotgun. But what interested Billy was that the hard-faced *hombre* Jeremiah Dandy, who had taken such an interest in him in the Bronco Saloon the night before, didn't show up either. This gave Billy considerable food for thought as he viewed the coming day's proceedings.

To the people from Freshwater Creek, the stage leaving for Laramie was something of an event. You never knew for sure who was leaving and who was coming and you could send a message to your kin through the company. Also it was good to watch the fine folk such as Miss Nancy Partridge and her tough old aunt mounting and taking their places in the best seats.

As Billy watched, there was a flutter and stir in the crowd and Miss Nancy Partridge herself sauntered towards the coach under the shade of a delicate parasol. This young woman sure is a dish, he thought, and probably spoiled some as well. Miss Emily, her aunt and chaperon, followed close behind, shaking off the flies with a fine yard of silk scarf. Though she too was tricked out in fine furbelows, Billy saw the face of a weatherbeaten old bird peering out from under her bonnet. and he guessed she had come up the hard way and seen a lot of life and it had shaped her into a tough old crow who knew when to perch and when to fly.

As she reached the coach, Miss Nancy paused and swept the crowd with her rather beautiful eyes as though looking for somebody to hand her on board. Several eager men hurried forward to oblige, but her eyes lighted on Billy and, before he could even stop to think, he had his hand on her elbow, helping her into the coach.

She turned in the doorway and smiled, the lovely fresh smile of an *ingénue*. 'Thank you, kind sir.'

'That's my pleasure, ma'am,' he said.

When Billy helped Miss Emily, the tough old crow, on board, he felt a stiffening in her arm and wondered momentarily whether she would bat him down like a pesky fly with her silk scarf.

'Thank you. Don't make a fuss,' she croaked harshly, as she stepped into the coach.

'You got the fancy touch there, boy, sure enough,' he heard old Jake laugh in his ear as he returned to the sidewalk. 'Ain't that just a fine piece of woman flesh?'

'Which one had you in mind?' Billy asked.

Old Jake wheezed with laughter.

'They do say the older the fiddle, the sweeter the tune,' he said.

'She's a beauty, ain't she, Billy?' a familiar voice said from close beside him.

Billy turned and it was Lou Lou with her hand resting lightly on his shoulder.

'Lou Lou!' he said. 'What are you doing here at this time of the morning?' It was a well-known fact that Lou Lou usually slept in till midday at least, but here she was with her face fixed nice and clean with no painted mask and no exaggerated lines, all dressed up pretty and neat to greet the sun. Without the mask of her make-up she looked remarkably pale, her face like dairy cream, and so clean and pure you might not recognize her as the girl in the Bronco Saloon.

'I just had to see you off, Billy,' she said quietly, so that nobody else could hear. 'And there's something I wanted to say to you after what happened last night.'

He glanced at her sideways. 'I didn't

like to see that cowboy pawing at you like that. The way you took off I thought you'd taken offence when I threw him out and spoiled your act.'

'You men,' she pouted. 'You never learn to understand a woman, do you? I was really touched by what you did there. It was so very dangerous and gallant. I just had to come down and tell you that this morning . . . before you leave.'

Billy smiled. He was going to say 'that's real kind' when someone shouted 'yahoo!' and the stage started to pull away. As he looked up, he saw Miss Nancy Partridge lean out of the window and smile and wave a handkerchief in his direction.

'She's real beautiful, ain't she, Billy?' Lou Lou whispered, with more than a hint of irony.

'She's a very neat young woman,' Billy said. He still felt the softness of Nancy's arm against his hand and he still had the scent of her perfume in his nostrils. It was kind of flower-like and reminded him of waving grasses and the cool open range when you were riding free.

'You couldn't be falling for that girl, could you?' Lou Lou asked, pressing against his arm.

'I don't think so,' he said. 'She probably lives in a palace anyway.'

'A cat can look at a queen,' she quipped. 'Pity you weren't riding shotgun after all,' she teased. 'You could have protected her from all those rough sweaty men.'

'I have other things on my mind, Lou Lou,' he said.

'I know that,' she replied more seriously, 'and that's another reason why I'm here.' She pressed herself gently against his arm. 'You know as well as I do, there's nothing happens in this town that nobody knows about. So take care, Billy. I hear that man Toms sittin' there quietly in the town gaol waitin' to be shipped is worse than a whole sack of rattlesnakes. Everyone knows about the havoc he's caused round about. And Toms doesn't ride alone. So you look after yourself, Billy, and don't do anything rash. You hear me?'

'I hear you,' he said. He thought of the hard-faced man Jeremiah Dandy sitting in on the card game and staring at him so intently.

Lou Lou gave his arm an affectionate squeeze. Billy felt a strange dryness in the throat he had rarely experienced before.

Gus Felixstowe had had them back up the other stage behind the sheriff's office and the gaol, so you just had to walk out through the door and climb into the cab.

When Billy arrived, a couple of men were standing guard with shotguns either side of the building and Gus Felixstowe was pacing up and down shaking his watch like a paunch-bellied Pickwick.

'Sooner we get this rig on the road the better it will be for everyone,' he muttered to Billy. 'You tooled up, son?'

Billy didn't care to be called 'son'. But he nodded and went into the office where Marshal Eldridge Leaver and Sheriff Watts were taking their breakfast, sitting each side of the office table. The sheriff's shooter was still on the table barrel pointing towards the iron bars of the gaol where Toms sat eating from a tin dish on his knees.

'Hi there, Billy!' Toms greeted in a high but gritty voice. 'See you got here on time. Why don't you take a bite of chow? They do a great breakfast here. Guess I could stay for the winter. How would that be, Sheriff?'

Sheriff Watts cackled. 'Glad to have you as my guest, Mr Toms. Sorry you have an appointment to keep with the hangman in Laramie. We wouldn't want to disappoint him none, would we now?'

'Don't you go and be too pessimistic, eh, Sheriff?' Toms shouted. 'Remember what they say about the cup and the lip.'

Sheriff Watts laughed again in his

own ugly way. 'There's going to be only one slip, Mr Toms, and that's the knot that sends you slipping down the chute to kingdom come with the rope around your neck.'

Marshal Leaver nodded and growled and turned as Billy checked a spare Winchester '73's action.

'Don't worry, Billy, there ain't no rust,' Toms declared. 'Sheriff Watts here keeps everything in the best of good order. Ain't that right, Sheriff?'

'That's right,' the sheriff concurred. 'We don't want hitches in the operation of the law, do we now?'

It was time to go. Marshal Leaver and Sheriff Watts scraped off their plates. The sheriff took up his shooter and held it low while the marshal turned the key and entered Toms's cell. Billy stood ready. He knew from experience that holding Toms was like gripping a river trout and a porcupine combined. But he was more interested in what might happen when they went out through the door.

'OK, gentlemen,' said Gus Felixs-towe, watch in hand from the entrance.

'OK, Mr Felixstowe,' Sheriff Watts replied, as Marshal Leaver urged Toms towards the door.

Billy knew Toms was a proud *hombre* as well as slippery yet he went up the steps and into the stage quiet as a mesmerized lamb. It made Billy feel kind of suspicious. He eased his gun in its holster, hoisted the Winchester on to his shoulder and climbed up on to the driver's seat of the coach.

This promises to be one hell of a trip, he thought, as the coach pulled away with its unsavoury cargo. Though he couldn't see any obvious reason why, he thought of Jeremiah Dandy's eyes boring into his back.

6

There's something a little crazy about this, Billy thought, as he took the stage out through the back of town. As though nobody is supposed to know we're leaving, though anyone who cares to see us can run across from the main drag and look for himself.

In fact, he saw eager faces clustered at the end of alleys, all wanting to catch a glimpse of the notorious badman Wesley Toms being taken off for trial and probably for the long drop in Laramie. There's always something awesome and compelling about a man facing his doom. Yet nobody saw as much as Toms's little finger since Marshal Leaver had drawn the dark grey curtains across. So the stage resembled a funeral carriage which in some ways added to the effect.

Billy was uneasy. Though he had seen

Marshal Leaver handcuff Toms to the handrail inside the coach, he felt that transporting the badman might be a tad too casual for safety and he kept recalling the hard-nosed visage of the man Jeremiah Dandy who had taken so much interest in him the night before in the Bronco Saloon. Had he really encountered this stranger before, he wondered? And was it in Colorado? And was it a face he should have remembered from a past he now regretted?

Another thing: why was he driving alone, perched high above the cab like a sitting duck waiting to be popped off for somebody's damned stew pot? Sure he had the Winchester '73 in its scabbard and the shotgun beside him on the floor, and sure, he had his Remington six-shooter snug and comfortable against his hip, yet why was there to be no relief driver when they reached Red Rock? It all smelled so much like stinking fish in a cooking kettle that he felt suspicion and anger in his craw as he drove the rig out through the back of town and hit the trail to Laramie further along.

Then again he pictured Eldridge Leaver and the sheriff eating their breakfast in the sheriff's office and remembered that the marshal and Toms even seemed comfortable together as though they were going on a Sunday School picnic or something. In the coach before he shut the door on them, he had heard Toms say to the Marshal, 'Well, as this might be the beginning of my doomsday, Marshal Leaver, why don't we share a little hooch or red eye together?'

'Thank you for the offer but I don't think so, Mr Toms,' the marshal had laughed. 'I think we'd both better keep sober and enjoy what we can see of the passing scenery. They say a man notices a lot more when it gets close to the Day of Judgement.'

'Too true, Marshal, too true,' Toms had rejoined, with pious irony like a latter-day Solomon.

Billy knew the two men were now sitting almost knee to knee inside the stage, Toms with his wrist secured to the bar and Leaver with his hand on his shooter. So there didn't seem much reason to fret about what was likely to happen from within, at least.

All the same he had another weird feeling — a sense of somebody following along the trail, not too close, yet not too far off and keeping out of sight. When he looked back he saw nothing, though, once or twice, there was a suggestion of dust rising along the top of the ridge and the clatter of rocks falling. So he knew in his bones he was right.

So he loosened the Winchester in its sheath and drove on.

Beyond the heads of his four horses, he could see the indentations from the hoofs and the wheel-marks from the other passenger stage that should be a good half an hour ahead of them.

The trail wound up through higher more densely wooded country with pines and cottonwoods — good cover for a bunch of bushwhackers. I sure am a sitting duck, he thought. A good marksman could put a bullet right through my brain with no trouble at all.

The feeling of being duped returned and this made him even angrier towards Gus Felixstowe and Sheriff Watts and the whole bunch of them. Don't get riled, boy, he said to himself. Stay cool and ready for whatever you need to do.

The trail curled in a loop and the ground fell away to the right through a tangle of trees and rocks, and suddenly he came upon it: the stagecoach propped against a tree, hanging loose over the edge of the drop, its passengers wandering in a daze and Miss Emily Partridge shouting and hollering and waving her arms about like a haunting banshee.

★　★　★

Billy drew his team to a halt and climbed down from the driving-seat. If this was part of a bushwhacking, it was a very complicated one. Marshal Leaver stuck his head out of the window.

'What happened?' he asked.

Before Billy could reply, the gambler Slam Beardsley loomed up before him. 'There's been an accident, Mr Bandro. That no-good driver of yours lost control and the coach pitched over the edge. We've been saved by nothing but a tree.'

'Sit tight, Marshal!' Billy advised, but Leaver already had the door open and was climbing down to survey the scene.

Now Toms stuck his head through the curtains. 'What gives here, Billy?' he asked.

'Stay there, Mr Leaver,' Billy advised. 'I'll go take a looksee.'

Billy went forward keeping a step behind Slam Beardsley. If this was a bushwhacking it was a very strange one. If Slam Beardsley was part of the deal Billy needed to keep him a step ahead and in sight.

He saw that the coach was in a very

precarious position, hanging over the drop like the carcass of a dead beast. One of the horses had smashed its skull against a tree; another lay thrashing with a broken leg, and the banker and the travelling salesman were trying to detach the other frightened horses from their harness and bring them on to the trail. Miss Emily Partridge went on hollering and roaring until her niece Nancy shouted, 'For God's sake, Aunt Emily! We're alive, aren't we? That's what matters.'

Well, she's a girl of spirit, anyway, Billy thought. But where was old Jake, the driver?

'The old man's somewhere's down there!' Slam Beardsley said, pointing down into the creek.

Billy saw his old friend almost immediately. Old Jake had been catapulted out of his driver's seat like a stone. He lay like a broken puppet halfway down the ravine — dead as a nail, where he had fallen like a ball from a sling.

Billy took charge of the whinnying

horses and tied them to a tree where they bucked and reared in their terror. Slam Beardsley, the gambler, started to calm the women and the three other frightened passengers. When the horses were secured and the injured one had been shot, Billy climbed down the ravine and took a look at Old Jake. It was clear from his twisted position that his body had been shaken up bad and his neck, as well as his arms, was broken. His eyes were still starting out with terror and his face was all bloody and mashed up where it had smashed against a rock.

'Is the poor man dead?' Miss Nancy pleaded.

'He's dead,' Billy said. 'I'm afraid he crossed the big divide. Didn't feel a thing.'

'Probably enjoyed the ride,' Slam Beardsley added, callously.

'I don't think so,' Billy said. 'It was short anyway.'

'What do we do now?' Marshal Leaver asked.

67

'Nothing we can do for Old Jake,' Billy said.

'I guess he drank too much in the Bronco last night,' Leaver declared.

'That's as maybe,' Billy said. He had always liked the old stagecoach driver and the sight of his twisted and broken body in the ravine caused him deep grief. But he knew he had to think in terms of practicalities. 'We can't do a thing about the coach. It's front wheel is smashed. Surprised nobody else got killed.'

'I have a duty to get my prisoner to Laramie,' the Marshal said, nervously fingering his gunbelt.

Toms still had his head stuck out of the window of the smaller coach. 'If I may make a suggestion, Marshal?' he said greasily.

'You're in no position to make suggestions to any man,' Marshal Leaver retorted hotly. 'If I may point it out, you're a prisoner under escort.'

'That's so,' Toms conceded. 'But you can't let those two charming ladies walk as far as Red Rock Station. Nor can they be expected to ride those terrified beasts. It ain't civilized. So I suggest we offer them and the other passengers refuge in this coach.'

'Oh, yeah. And what do we do with you, Toms?' Leaver mocked.

'Well, since the respectable passengers won't want to be contaminated by a man going to trial, you and me could ride the spare horses bare-back Injun style, as far as Red Rock Station.'

Leaver ran his fingers over his stubbly chin and considered. Billy wasn't concerned either way. Having Marshal Leavers and Toms riding alongside the coach to Red Rock Station might even be considered an advantage since he could look down on them and keep some semblance of control.

'I think we have to do that,' Leaver concluded. He unlocked the cuffs and tied Toms securely with his arms in front of him and hoisted him up on one of the most docile horses so he could ride behind him on another horse. Both rode alongside the stage horses where

Billy could look down and cover them.

'This is the worst journey I ever took in my life!' Miss Emily clucked harshly. 'I knew I should have asked my brother to send his men down to escort us.'

'Auntie!' Miss Nancy objected. 'There's a man dead down there. We have to show some respect.'

Miss Emily sniffed her disdain and Billy helped her up the steps into the smaller coach. Then, as he put his hand on Nancy Partridge's arm, she turned and smiled. 'Thank you for rescuing us, Mr Bandro. Such a pity about that poor driver. He seemed such a good man.'

'He was a good man, Miss Partridge,' Billy affirmed.

Miss Nancy had a look of real sadness and concern on her face. But she was stronger than she looked. Billy thought that was a good thing because she might need every ounce of her strength later.

She glanced down at him and he nodded. Suddenly he knew he must get that rig to Red Rock and maybe as far as Laramie through hell or high water.

7

As he drove, Billy thought again about the man with the face of hickory wood and, though it was only a hunch, kept imagining him as the mysterious rider trailing them along the high ground.

Below him, he could see Marshal Leaver jogging along beside the coach and just a little further ahead Toms with the rope running back to Leaver. This smaller coach had been too cramped to hold all the passengers and their accompanying baggage. So the two ladies, the banker and the travelling salesman were inside, and the gambler Slam Beardsley was perched beside him next to the driver's seat. Beardsley's rather fancy presence with his gold watch chain and his ring-festooned fingers increased Billy's unease. Why should a gambler who spent most of his waking hours in dark saloons cheating at poker want to sit next to the driver of a stage, especially when there might be considerable danger, even if he did carry a Smith & Wesson underneath his fancy jacket? Yet Beardsley seemed friendly enough in a wry, tight-lipped kind of way.

'Good to have the chance to talk to you again, Billy,' he chimed, as they trundled along, 'even if it is at the expense of that old fool who broke his neck back there.'

'He did hit the bottle too hard,' Billy conceded, 'but he wasn't an old fool. He was a good man and a good old buddy.'

'Pity we couldn't stop and bury him,' Slam Beardsley said nonchalantly.

'You take your chance out here,' Billy said. 'They'll send a rig back from Red Rock to pick up what's left of the body after the coyotes have finished with it, and they'll give him a grand funeral at Freshwater.'

He pictured the little staging post at Red Rock Station with its cluster of buildings: a miniature saloon, not much more than a shack with a single room; stables where the Walker horses were kept; a minute trading post where the Cheyenne, the Crow, and other tribes came to barter and trade. On a lonely mast a single tattered flag flew: the old duster with its circle of stars.

As Billy was thinking about this, Toms glanced up over his shoulder and leered.

'You did a noble piece of work there, Billy,' he shouted back. 'I feel real proud of the way you handled the situation with the wrecked coach. You still got some sand in your craw after all.'

'That was all in the line of duty, Mr Toms,' Billy replied sarcastically. Billy glanced at the gambler who gave him a sceptical grin.

'I did hear rumours you rode with Toms one time?' he murmured quietly. 'He still seems to have a torch of friendship for you.'

'Where'd you pick that up — riding with him?' Billy growled between his teeth.

'Floating in the air,' Slam Beardsley grinned. 'We all carry unwanted baggage around with us, stuff we'd like to shake off and drop along the trail.'

Billy thought, things have changed a deal since I rode with that ornery critter.

'Let me tell you something straight,' Billy muttered. between his teeth, 'I once saw that smooth-talking sidewinder gun a man down in cold blood and it wasn't a pretty sight.'

'That so?' Beardsley raised his eyebrows. 'So you reckon he's earned the long drop in Laramie? Is that what you're saying?'

Billy pursed his lip and noticed Beardsley patting the Smith & Wesson on his thigh like a man who valued an old friend.

'I'm saying I do my duty, Mr Beardsley, and I don't ever want to see another man die like that.'

Beardsley shook his head thoughtfully. 'Does it occur to you that this is a mighty strange way to convey a smooth varmint like that to his trial? A single marshal and a bunch of passengers on a public stagecoach? Seems kinda careless to me.'

Billy buttoned his lip and said nothing. He knew the gambler spoke sense and it made him feel like a fool. He was still chewing on his anger as they approached Red Rock Station. The gambler's words rang in his ear and that made him even more alert than usual. So, as they drew near the station, he watched out for signs and immediately saw something that made his hair prick under his Stetson.

'That flag,' he muttered. 'You see that flag on the mast?'

'I see the old red flag fluttering there,' Slam Beardsley grinned. 'What about it?'

'Something ain't right about it. It's trailing half way down the mast, that's what's about it.'

'I see what you mean.' Beardsley's hand was on the Smith & Wesson in its holster.

Billy hollered out suddenly and drew in the horses. The coach came to a slithering halt, Miss Emily Partridge shouted out something and, below him, Marshal Leaver drew and cocked his shooter. 'What's with you, Billy?' he shouted.

Billy raised himself from his driving seat and surveyed the little cluster of buildings. Something was definitely wrong, something more than a drooping flag at half mast. At this distance he could usually see Bud Weaver waving at the window, or waiting on the porch to welcome them in. But the windows were dark and vacant as the dead eyes of a corpse and nothing stirred.

Another thing too — the thing that decided him. Way to the right behind them he caught the flicker of a single rider.

'I was right. That's him,' Billy breathed. 'The man with the face like a hickory carving — Jeremiah Dandy.'

'Is that right?' Slam Beardsley said grimly.

Billy pulled the whole outfit around in a big half circle so that the horses faced a low range of scree-strewn hills a couple of hundred yards to the west.

'We're going for that scree!' he shouted. He swung his whip and lashed the rump of the lead horse. 'Get up there!'

As the stage gathered speed, Billy looked over his shoulder and saw what he expected to see. A number of riders burst suddenly from the cover of the buildings. The puffs of smoke from their weapons told him the stagecoach was under fire.

★ ★ ★

There wasn't a hope he could outride a dozen determined men on horseback and he knew it. He pulled the coach up tight to the scree-strewn hillside and turned. The riders — ten, he counted — were galloping forward with hair-raising speed. They caught us like a bunch of rats in a barn! he thought. But

Slam Beardsley had other ideas. He had grabbed the Winchester '73 from its sheath and spreadeagled himself on top of the stage. Before Billy could speak, the gambler had pumped off three rounds at the approaching riders.

'Get that one, you bastard, get that one!' he shouted, as one of the riders threw up his arm and rolled off his horse into the dust. The other riders checked and fanned out right and left, still firing recklessly at the coach. Billy leapt down over the side and yanked open the door. With the Remington in his right hand, he grabbed the nearest passenger and jerked him out of the coach.

'Get up among the rocks under cover of the coach!' he shouted. 'Get up there and get your heads down!'

They popped out like corks from a bottle, the banker and the travelling salesman, battling with one another in the doorway, the two women leaping white-faced into his arms. Emily Partridge blasphemed like a man and Nancy

78

submitted to his pull with a strange confidence he fleetingly admired.

'Get up behind the boulders and lie still!' he shouted. 'Keep your heads down!'

He turned and fired a couple of quick shots at the circling riders, but they were still too far off for the six-shooter to be effective.

Suddenly he was aware of Eldridge Leaver hustling Toms at gun-point. 'You try to make a move and I'll shoot you dead!' he shouted.

That was when the horses went mad and bolted with the coach.

The driverless coach rattled on for a hundred yards and then careened on to its side with the horses screaming and floundering in the dust. Slam Beardsley had been lying on the roof pumping shots at the riders, but, as the coach tipped over, he disappeared in a cloud of dust.

Now the riders were circling closer — close enough to distinguish and recognize faces. Billy saw the man with the hickory face and the fancy saddle rein in and level his gun. He brought his Remington into play a moment too late.

There was a flash like the whole sky was bursting with lightning before darkness swept over the horizon and he fell like a dead man and knew no more.

8

His head was bust open like a melon. Busted and broken right through to the core. Yet he felt the coolness of living water on his face and he suddenly started into consciousness.

'Take it easy,' the voice said. 'Don't move too quickly!'

Move! His whole body seemed paralysed. Every time he twitched a muscle, his head screamed like a demon!

'What happened!' he shouted, in a voice like a cry from the depths of hell.

'Easy, boy. Take a drink.' The guardian angel hoisted him gently into position and trickled tepid water between his lips.

It helped. Suddenly he knew where he was, among the rocks supported by a shape he dimly recognized.

'Lie still,' Slam Beardsley said. 'Lie still till I get you under cover.'

'What happened?' he asked again, as the rocks came into sharp focus and the sun blazed into his eyes.

'You got hit is what happened,' Beardsley growled. 'I thought you were dead meat till you thrashed out at me. A slug creased you on the skull. Only a crease. Not even a dent. You've got a tough skull. Another inch over and you'd be a dead man.' His voice seemed to echo in Billy's head like a shout in a great cavern and he could still hear a strange droning noise like a giant hornet buzzing in his head.

Yet he sat up with the gambler supporting his back. 'What happened to all those passengers?' he said.

'Didn't trust me, did you?' Beardsley said. 'Thought I was there to help that ugly critter Toms escape. That's what you thought.'

Billy held his head gently between his hands as though trying to ease it back into place. His hand came away wet with blood.

'Gotta get that head tied up good

and clean,' the gambler said. Though his voice was harsh and even sardonic, his deft fingers showed unusual concern. With some difficulty and a deal of help Billy hoisted himself up on to his feet. As he limped towards the buildings of the Red Rock Station, his head began to clear so he could see better and think straighter.

'What happened to all the people? Those two women?' he mumbled. The abandoned coach lay half on its side and a spooky silence hung over the rocky hillside. Beardsley must have jumped clear before it fell. The horses were beating the air frantically with their hoofs.

'What happened was we were dealing with a bunch of ruthless killers here,' Beardsley muttered. 'When I fell off the coach I managed to fall on my toes. So it could have been worse. But I knew I hadn't a snowball in hell's chance of beating off those killers. So I crawled off and hid up among the rocks like you said. You were lucky.

They killed Marshal Leavers with no more concern than swatting a fly. Shot him right through the head. Would have given you the same treatment. But the way you were lying, wallowing in your blood, fooled them and they took you for dead. If you'd twitched a muscle that man with the hard face would have put another bullet through your head. He was going to but Toms stopped him.' Beardsley gave a sinister chuckle. 'Said he wanted to remember you beautiful like you used to be.'

As they moved on, Billy saw the marshal lying like a twisted dummy on his side, eyes staring sightlessly at the sky and half his head blown away.

'Poor bastard,' he said.

'He didn't realize how ruthless Toms was,' Beardsley said. 'Otherwise he'd have taken a deal more care. That man was stupid and you can't afford to be stupid in this territory.'

'What about the other passengers?' Billy asked again. 'I don't see those two women.'

'I didn't see anything more of that banker character or the travelling salesman. I guess they managed to scuttle away like a couple of scorpions and hide. There's an awful lot of heavy scree up there.'

'What about those two women?' Billy insisted.

Beardsley was ominously silent for a moment. 'You could say they weren't so lucky,' he said. 'You can't run too fast with all that heavy skirting material round your legs. So Toms just herded them together and carried them off. I guess he thought there was a ransom in it.' He paused. 'Maybe something more, too.'

The possible fate of Nancy Partridge and her aunt brought Billy into full consciousness with a jolt. 'We can't let them go like that,' he said.

'Not much you can do about it in your condition,' Beardsley said.

'They can't have got far. We can go after them,' Billy shouted. He spun round to look where Toms and his men had gone and his head rattled like it was full of rocks in a landslide and he almost passed out again.

'Steady there!' Beardsley held on to him.

'We gotta go after them,' Billy said. He could see the faint diminishing dots of riders in a cloud of dust way off to the right.

'Maybe we do,' Beardsley said. 'But right now we got to stop and think.'

Billy knew he was right. He lay among the rocks for a while trying to recover. Beardsley brought him a canteen of water and he drank.

'You may be right, about going after Toms and his bunch,' he said, 'but right now you're in no condition to commit suicide and neither am I. But I'll tell you one thing: Emily Partridge screamed and kicked out a bit but it didn't do any good. The hard man just swung her up on to a horse's back.'

'What about Miss Nancy?'

'Well . . . ' Beardsley's mouth twisted in a grin. 'That young woman might be refined, but she sure got some guts. I never heard such bad language from a woman in all my life, and that's the truth.'

★　★　★

When Billy felt ready, they gathered their strength and moved towards the buildings of Red Rock Station and Billy saw at once why Bud Weaver hadn't come out to greet them. The old man was perched on his chair, gagged and trust up like a chicken ready for the oven. Close beside him lay the body of Cliff Franklin, his assistant, shot through and through like a colander.

Beardsley took out his Bowie knife, sawed through the gag, and cut the old man free.

'By God, I tried to warn you, Billy,' Weaver shrilled. 'When I saw them coming I pulled the flag down to half mast. But they just stormed the place and tied everybody up. 'Cept poor Cliff there. He made the mistake of reaching for his gun. They plugged him at least six times. He didn't stand a chance, poor kid.'

Billy could see from the body that six times was an underestimation. 'What about the other hands?'

'I guess they're trussed up too, unless they managed to hide some place. Looks like you need doctoring yourself. Sit down here, son, and let me see about that wound.'

Apart from being a friend, Bud Weaver was well known as a local medico. So he examined Billy's wound, poured whiskey on it which stung like hell, and bound him up with clean bandages. 'You were lucky there, boy,' he said. 'Creased you right above the ear. Bone must have deflected it round. A more acute angle and you'd have found your glory day.'

Slam Beardsley went in search of the other hands, and found two shivering with terror and bound up like swaddling babes. A third emerged from a hayloft with his hands in the air. At the same moment, the banker and the travelling salesman crept up to the door and Slam swung round with the Smith & Wesson in his hand and nearly gunned them down.

'It's OK!' the terrified banker said, with his hands in the air. 'We come in peace.'

'There's riders coming in from the Sweetwater direction.' The travelling salesman pointed a wavering finger off to his right. 'Maybe they're coming back to finish us off, the butchers!'

9

Everyone crowded to the window. There was a rider, certainly. In fact there were three riders making their way cautiously towards the buildings of Red Rock Station. Although Billy was still suffering from double vision, he squinted, then closed one eye and gave his judgement. 'That's Sheriff Watts,' he announced.

It was Watts, sure enough. He rode high and proud, wearing the big black Stetson he always wore. With him, a little to the rear, were two others Billy recognized, part-time cowboys who mostly lay around waiting till round-up time. Now they looked spruced up and ready for action, though from past experience Billy knew better. One of the cowboys was the man he had thrown out of the Bronco Saloon when he had tried to molest Lou Lou and who had attempted to draw on him. He was lucky Billy hadn't shot him down in self-defence.

Watts reined in and dismounted with as much leisurely dignity as his fat paunch would allow and with his carbine cradled against his chest. 'Goodday, Mr Weaver. How you doin?' he asked in a tone of irony.

Bud Weaver spat a stream of tobacco juice into the dust, and growled, 'How I'm doin ain't good, Sheriff. In fact it's far from dandy.'

As he started to describe the events of the day, the two deputies — for that's what Billy concluded they were now — dismounted and strode on to the porch, looking important. The cowboy he had thrown out of the saloon stared straight ahead as though refusing to recognize him but Billy saw a sneer at the corner of his mouth.

Sheriff Watts turned his attention to Billy. 'Looks like you got shot, Billy.' Though he clucked like an old hen Billy noted he didn't look greatly concerned.

The cowboy Billy had tangled with gave a low cackle of derision.

Billy stared straight back at Watts. He didn't nod and he didn't treat the sheriff to his usual amiable grin. 'There's another man shot inside here,' he said. 'They killed that boy Cliff Franklin. And you'll find Eldridge Leaver lying up there close to the stage staring up at the sun. And there's several of Wesley Toms's men lying dead close by.'

'Well, that's real bad,' Watts concluded, 'especially about Eldridge Leaver. He was a real nice guy. He should have taken a deal more care. I told him nobody could ever trust a man like Toms but he wouldn't listen none.'

'Too nice,' Billy said, 'And I agree he was a mite too stupid.' Every time he spoke his head felt like a cavern full of tumbling rocks.

'What brought you here, Sheriff?' Beardsley asked suddenly.

Sheriff Watts gave him a cool and suspicious look. 'Somebody rode into

Sweetwater. They came across the wrecked coach with the busted wheel back there and they found the body of Jake at the bottom of the ravine. So I took it as my duty to ride out and take a peek since Eldridge Leaver had Wesley Toms under escort to Laramie. And it seems I was right, don't it?' He hitched his thumbs into his belt and eased it across his capacious belly.

'If you'd been here a little earlier, Sheriff,' Billy said, 'we might have fought off those killers. Now they got clean away and they took those two ladies from Laramie with them.'

Watts bit his lip and frowned. 'That's bad. Partridge owns the biggest spread up Laramie way and he won't be none too pleased. He could make big trouble if we don't get them back mighty quick.'

'And there could be a lot more trouble with Wesley Toms and his bunch of killers on the loose,' Weaver put in. 'The way they killed Cliff, those animals will stop at nothing.'

Sheriff Watts played with the buckle of his belt and, though he still smiled, Billy saw that he was uneasy.

'So what do you intend to do, Sheriff?' he demanded.

The muscles on Watts's jaw tightened. 'What we do, Billy, is we take you back to Sweetwater to get the evidence and sort this mess out.'

'That ain't going to help those two women much,' Slam Beardsley growled. 'If we're going to be any good to them, we got to get after them now before the trail goes cold. If we want to free those ladies and bring Toms in we've got to act pronto.'

The sheriff's eyebrows shot up with astonishment. Then he eyed the gambler in the fancy clothes and the gold rings with suspicion and contempt. 'I wouldn't have thought chasing outlaws on the trail was quite your style, Mr Beardsley, you being more of a gambling man.'

Beardsley chuckled and drew his hand across his moustache. 'I got more style than you got hairs on your chest, Mr Watts. If you care to take a looksee at those bodies lying out there, you'll notice Toms's men have been drilled quite neat with Winchester '73 shells where I dropped them.'

'That's as maybe,' Sheriff Watts said, with a slight jeer in his voice. 'You may be a good shootist, mister, but it don't make no never mind to me. I'm afraid I still have to ask you and Billy here to come back to Sweetwater with me so we can sort this thing out proper in the eyes of the law. We got a serious situation here. Two stages wrecked. The Walker Company ain't going to like that one little bit. And then there's the killing of Marshal Leaver to consider. Not to mention the snatching of those two ladies. This is a matter for the judge to look into. And that's what we must do.' He turned to his assistants for support. 'So I'm afraid we got to take you two gentlemen into custody.'

'That's the truth, Bandro,' the cowboy jeered. 'We got to take you in.'

'What the hell you raving about?' Billy fired up. 'You go out there and look beyond that pile of flint and you'll still see the dust rising where those killers are riding away with the two women. We got to get after them now. That's what we must do.'

'Steady on there, Billy!' The sheriff held up his hand like he was a wise counsellor about to deliver judgement. 'I'm afraid the law means something around here. You got to come back to Sweetwater with us. I have to insist on it.'

The two part-time deputies made a move towards Billy and Slam Beardsley. Billy saw the grin of pleasure on the face of the one he had thrown out of the saloon. But before the two deputies could lay a finger on either of them, Slam Beadsley had drawn and cocked his shooter.

'Not one inch closer, if you don't mind, gentlemen.' His eyes narrowed down to fine slits and he crouched like a well-oiled killing machine.

The two cowboys froze and drew back. Sheriff Watts's brows came together and he nodded. 'So that's the way you want it to be.' He glanced at Billy. 'Is that the way you want it, Billy?'

Billy felt Slam Beardsley close beside him, taut as a bowstring. 'That ain't the way I want it, Mr Watts, but that's the way it must be if you insist on taking us back to Freshwater instead of going after that killing bunch.'

Watts looked him over with critical contempt. 'You know what you're doing, Billy? This here gambling man has a reputation down south in Texas. Ain't that so, Beardsley?'

There was a moment's tense silence before the gambler shrugged. 'I had a few brushes with the law down that way, that's true, Mr Watts. But I never killed an innocent man and I haven't fallen short in my obligations yet. I agree with Billy. If we don't get after Toms and his band of killers right now, we might as well let the whole thing go.' He shrugged again. 'Best thing, Mr

Watts, is for you to team up with us and get this thing over soon as maybe.'

It wasn't a bad suggestion. Until now, Billy had had nothing in particular against Watts though he knew Watts had a grudge against him for some reason. But he was far less certain of the two deputies, one of whom had stupid eyes. The one he had thrown out of the saloon was itching to come back on him — he could see that clearly. He didn't fancy riding with either of them, especially against a killing bunch like Toms's men and Jeremiah Dandy.

But before he could make another bid for common sense, the sheriff shook his head. 'Nothing doing, Mr Beardsley, nothing doing. I'm taking you in and that's flat. And you'd better put that shooter away, because pointing that thing at me is strictly against the law and it won't do you no good.'

Billy paused for a moment and then took a big decision. 'OK then, Mr Watts. You don't leave us much choice.' He drew his Remington and covered

Watts. 'I'll have to ask you to unbuckle your gunbelts and let your weapons drop on to the floor.'

Watts and his two assistants held off for a moment. The one he had floored in the saloon was trying to make up his mind to go for his gun and he swayed to and fro like a cougar torn between attacking and retreating.

Watts looked angry and perplexed. 'You can't do that, Bandro. Not without opening yourself to the suspicion you're helping Toms to make his break.'

'That's a funny way to figure it, Watts,' Billy said. 'I might have ridden with Toms one time but there's no love between us now. And those two women were in my care. So I owe them the best deal I can give them. I figure you're throwing away our chances of catching those murdering killers.'

Watts eyed him like a snake eyeing a prairie rabbit.

'You're doing a damned fool thing here, Bandro, and you're going to suffer for it if you don't put that gun back in its holster. You know that?'

Billy kept the Remington on Watts. 'That's as maybe, Watts. That's as maybe. Now get those belts unbuckled and lay those irons on the ground real slowly.'

Watts stared into his eyes with steady contempt for a moment. Then he unbuckled his gunbelt and let it slide to the ground. Slam Beardsley still had his gun trained on the deputies. The leary cowboy looked paler than a stained wagon cover and mad as hell. Yet he followed the sheriff's example with a growl of complaint.

'And now, Mr Weaver,' Billy said. 'I'll have to ask you to oblige me by tying these three gentlemen real tight to three good chairs and keep them snug until after we ride out.'

Weaver looked somewhat abashed.

'I'm warning you, Weaver,' Watts said. 'You do any such tying you'll be answerable to the law.'

'Good point,' Billy agreed. 'In which case I'll do it myself.'

He trussed up Watts and the two deputies tight as turkeys ready for the market.

'You'll pay for this, Bandro,' the cowboy said between his teeth.

'That don't make no never mind,' Billy said.

10

Bud Weaver looked real nervy about the tying up, but while Slam Beardsley stood guard over the prisoners he and Billy went outside to stock up the saddle-bags with beans and jerky and other provisions.

'I hope you know what you're brewing up fer yerselves, young feller,' Weaver said. 'That gambling man might have helped you out of a deal of trouble, but he might not be all he pretends to be. You could be jumping like a catfish clean into scalding water. Did that occur to you, Billy?'

Billy placed his hand on Weaver's shoulder. 'That gambling man probably saved my life,' he said.

'Well,' Bud Weaver insisted, 'he might be good with a shooter, but I wouldn't trust a man with fancy rings on his fingers and a tendency to cheat at the card table.'

'If it hadn't been for him,' Billy said 'I might be lying staring at the sun like Marshal Leaver. You know that?'

'I guess you do have a point there,' the old man conceded. 'But what you're doing here is on the wrong side of the law and you could pay dear for that. It ain't healthy to rile up Sheriff Watts like that. He could come down on you awful hard after I untie him when you've gone after those desperate men,' Weaver said. 'Have you thought about what Sheriff Watts might do when he gets free? He's not gonna like you one little bit for making him look like a turkey.'

'He only looks like a turkey because he's behaving like a turkey,' Billy said.

'Another thing,' the old man insisted. 'How do you think two riders are going to beat up on a ruthless gang like Toms has got? Toms and that straight-shootin' buddy of his won't hardly make nothing of killing you two and frying you up for breakfast. You know that?'

Billy squeezed his arm. 'I'll face that

when the time comes, old buddy.' What the old man said had some sense in it, but Billy had made up his mind. 'I'm going after Toms,' he said. 'There are no two ways about it. Someone's got to go after him and free those two women. By the time Watts gets on to the job, the trail will be dead cold. And Toms will have got clean away. Remember this, old-timer: when I climbed into the driving seat of that rig I took on the responsibility of getting Toms and then those other passengers to Laramie. I take that as a kind of solemn duty.'

Bud Weaver grunted and they went into the stables to pick out four good saddle horses.

'That's real noble, Billy, and danged fool-hardy, I grant you that,' Weaver agreed. 'And if'n you're dead set on killing yerself, you can't do better than this chestnut and the sorrel.' He spoke quietly as though Sheriff Watts might be listening through a crack in the wall. Billy noticed that the old guy had become a lot more friendly out of sight and sound of the sheriff. 'But, I got to emphasize this, Billy: you're taking a big chance here. I agree with your motives, but goin' against the law like this can be a fool's errand, especially with a partner you might not be able to trust. When they catch up on you, you know what will happen, don't yer?'

'What will happen, old-timer?'

'Cut out the 'old-timer' crap, Billy. I seen a lot of things in my days. And I've seen good and well-intentioned men swinging like over-ripe fruit from high trees. Are you sure these two women you're intent on rescuing are worth the trouble? Ask me, they probably gave Toms and those killers the eye and that's why they took 'em like that.'

He turned and gave Billy a toothless grin and a lopsided wink.

Billy was not amused. He remembered a magic moment the night before when he had stood and looked up at the balcony of the hotel and seen Nancy Partridge looking down at him, the friendly way she had spoken and the rare feelings he'd had because of it. He also remembered helping her up into the stagecoach and the smell of her perfume.

'Keep your dirty thoughts to yourself, Bud!' he snapped. 'And thanks for the provisions and the horses.'

★   ★   ★

They rode out together, Slam Beardsley and Billy, and picked up the trail left by the outlaws without difficulty.

'The old man won't waste time before freeing Watts,' Slam Beardsley said. 'He can't afford to lose credit with the law.'

Billy knew Beardsley was right but, as they rode on, he was still trying to figure why Beardsley was so hot for the chase.

'How come you're riding along with me?' he said. 'You'd be a dang sight better off making your way up to Laramie. They say there's good pickings up there, and with your skills you could be a rich dude.'

Slam Beardsley looked at him sideways and grinned, showing his gold teeth. 'Life has more than money in its saddle-bag, Billy,' he said. 'And anyway, I like your company. You got grit, you know that?'

'Never thought much about it,' Billy said. Like many men who had lived by their wits on the trail he had no taste for flattery.

'I don't think you trust me yet,' Beardsley said, turning in the saddle to flash his gold teeth again.

Billy didn't deny the fact. He couldn't reason why a gambling man who could rake in money in every saloon in the territory should waste his time and risk his hide chasing a bunch of outlaws, especially when he stood a good chance of getting himself strung up or shot.

'I'm not sure I trust any man,' he admitted. 'And you have no reason to trust me either 'specially since I once rode with Toms.'

Beardsley inclined his head. 'That's true and that's what fascinates me. Like you fell in with Toms for some good reason of your own. And I don't wish to fathom that. I guess it's none of my business.' He raised his head. 'As for my motives, I can't explain, Billy. Sure, I'm a gambler. Always have been. That's my nature and my way. That's what I was trying to tell you back in the Bronco Saloon. But even gamblers sometimes have a sense of what's right. We could be partners, you an' me. Life is a plum, you know, begging to be plucked. What do you say, Billy? Let's team up until this mess is over and then think about it again.'

'I'll settle for that,' Billy said.

Slam Beardsley turned in the saddle and extended his hand.

Billy took the hand and grasped it firmly. 'Until this mess is over,' he said. 'We've got a lot of hard riding to do especially with Toms in front of us and Watts tailing behind us.'

'That damned fat-headed fool!' Beardsley exclaimed. 'You really think he will tail us?'

Billy looked back along the trail. 'I guess not. Watts hasn't got enough sand.'

Beardsley grinned. 'That's a shame,' he said. 'Because we're being damned fools going after that bunch, just the two of us. You know that?'

Billy grinned back. 'Two against how many?' he said.

'I make it eight, but there could be more,' Beardsley said. 'I guess that makes four each . . . and there might be more.'

'Just as long as we have enough grit we can do it,' Billy said, with a confidence he didn't necessarily feel.

*　*　*

The sun was already riding low like a red faced comanchero when they came to the river and knew they must cross. The horse tracks they were following went right down to the brink.

Billy dismounted and counted six sets of tracks, and shook his head. 'With the two we killed back there at Red Rock that makes eight. There's only six crossing here. That suggests two peeled off.'

He mounted again and they wheeled their horses and scouted along the bank, looking for more signs.

'Here.' Billy dismounted and knelt close to the soft mud in the fading light. 'Yeah, two peeled off here and the rest went across back there. You know what that means?'

Beardsley had also dismounted and stood with his shoulder close to his horse's flank. 'It could mean they mean to drop us as we cross,' he said in a quiet monotone.

'Could be,' Billy said. 'If we stay here like sitting ducks we'll be dead ducks. That means Toms is expecting us to follow. I guess it might be healthy to move right now.'

11

'What do we do now?' Slam Beardsley spoke low.

'What we do,' Billy said, 'is get away from the river before they shoot us down.'

They wheeled their mounts and rode back from the river to a stand of trees and brushwood that would give them reasonable cover, and beyond which was a low bluff.

They tethered their horses to a small tree and took up a good viewing position. There was series of bluffs overlooking the river which might provide a good place to shoot down on a man crossing the river. The sun was sitting very low in the trees and it would soon be dark.

'What we do,' Billy said, 'is we wait till dark and move further off up there and make camp for the night away from the river.'

When full darkness came and the moon began to peer through the trees they moved stealthily further up to higher ground. They hobbled the horses where they could graze and made camp.

'They could pick us off here like two dummies in a fair-ground,' Slam Beardsley muttered.

''Cept we won't be here,' Billy said quietly.

'I see,' Beardsley said. 'The old campfire trick. You think they'll fall for it?'

'They might and they might not.' Billy laughed. 'Like you said, we have to learn to take a chance.'

So they built a camp-fire and spread their bedrolls and, while Slam Beardsley stood guard, listening for the sound of breaking twigs and heavy breathing, Billy stuffed the bedrolls with rocks so they looked like men sleeping by a camp-fire.

'You did a good job there, Billy,' Beardsley whispered, as they climbed the hill and settled down behind some rocks. 'Those two guys down there are sleeping like they're waiting for the crack of doom.'

Billy gave a low laugh. 'Which is on its way.'

They got down on their stomachs and strained their eyes through the darkness towards the river. The stars started to twinkle and the moon edged up behind a bluff and everything seemed as quiet and peaceable as a scene in a romantic novel.

Billy took a swig from his water bottle and passed it on to Beardsley. Then he handed him a hunk of jerky. 'This isn't much but it's a whole lot healthier than a bullet or a ball in the head,' he said.

For a time they munched in silence. Then, though there wasn't enough light for Beardsley to see the gold hunter he carried in his vest pocket, they divided the night into watches and settled down. Beardsley took the first session and he arranged himself behind a rock with the Winchester trained on the camp-fire in the clearing below. Billy lay with his chin in his hat, the Remington close to his face. It was sort of spooky, especially when the coyotes set up their eerie wailing along the river-bank. But Billy had had one hell of a day, especially with the bullet grazing his skull, and he fell into a deep sleep almost immediately.

* * *

He woke like an animal that knows it's being stalked. Slam Beardsley stuck an elbow into Billy's face. He eased himself up to peer over the boulder to where the gambler was jabbing his finger.

'They're on their way,' he whispered hoarsely.

At first Billy could hear and see nothing, though the moon was bathing the scene below in a blue eerie light. Then there was a faint movement that seemed no more than the wind rustling through the low junipers. Slam Beardsley cocked the Winchester and held it steady, supported it on the rock. An age seemed to pass and Billy might have thought his imagination had been working overtime before there was another faint stirring below and the unmistakable silhouette of a crouching man close to the bushes where the bedrolls lay like sleeping men.

Then there was a long pause before the figure began to inch closer to the ground and crawl forward towards the apparently peaceful men by the campfire.

'They took the bait,' Billy breathed, as the figure raised itself slightly . . . just enough to cover its intended target no more than ten feet away from it.

'He's good,' Beardsley whispered. 'He creeps and crawls like an Indian. You gotta be good on your last mission.' He shook with laughter under his breath and raised the Winchester a little higher.

But before he could fire, one of the

horses whinnied and the others stirred and began to wheel and Billy knew that the other outlaw was down there trying to cut them loose.

The two guns fired almost simultaneously, the one from below in the bushwhacker's hand, and the one above from the Winchester held steady against Beardsley's cheek. Billy saw the flash from the outlaw's gun and then saw it leap from his hand as he clutched his chest and lurched up and backwards into the bushes.

He didn't wait. 'You got him!' he said, as he leapt up from behind the rock and scrambled forward, not toward the camping place but toward the stand of trees where the horses were hobbled. Luckily the four horses, the two they had ridden and the two spares, were spaced out. So the man who was intent on cutting them loose might not have an easy time.

As Billy scrambled and jolted down between rocks and scrubby bushes, he kept the Remington pushed out before him. He heard Beardsley scrambling down behind him with the same purpose . . . to save the horses.

Now he could see the shadowy figure moving among the animals, trying to get one horse away and flee on its back. Suddenly, at the last moment, having heard the shot that had apparently drilled his companion, he pulled back and leapt on the horse he had managed to cut loose. Billy knelt quickly and steadied his arm for a quick shot. The Remington bucked in his hand, but he knew he hadn't a chance of a snowball in hell of winging the man at that distance. So he scrambled on, knowing Beardsley would also pause and loose one off with the much more effective Winchester.

As Beardsley took his shot, the horse bucked quickly, the other horses began to whirl in panic, and the rider almost slid from its back.

Billy continued to run as he saw the outlaw grab at the horse's mane and cling on.

'You got lucky there!' Billy said, as he crouched to aim again. But he didn't fire because he knew it would be wasting a bullet. Beardsley obviously thought the same, because he came and sat, panting beside Billy.

'I guess that one won't come back in a hurry,' he said. 'Pity he got one of the horses.'

After they'd paused to catch their breath, they approached the camp-fire cautiously. Billy was pretty sure the man Beardsley had hit was either severely disabled or dead, but you could never be sure.

There was no doubt when they came upon the man lying with his arms out straight in the bushes. Beardsley had hit him clean through the heart.

Billy was busy scooping the bushwhacker's gun from the bushes and unbuckling his gunbelt. There was useful ammunition there. He looked down at the dead face and saw it wasn't the visage of the hard-faced man Jeremiah who had followed the stage from Sweetwater Creek.

★ ★ ★

Though they guessed the man who had gone for the horses wouldn't be crazy enough or have enough sand to come back, they went to calm the three horses in case they injured themselves. Then they stamped out what was left of the fire, gathered together their gear, and rode off to another place to pitch their camp.

12

Though it was time to sleep, the two men felt as prickly as cactus, and though Billy's head was aching like someone was rolling a rock in his skull, he couldn't settle down.

There was something about this bushwhacking down by the river that wasn't quite right. As though Wesley Toms knew he would be tailed even though Marshal Leavers had been killed and *I've taken a bullet in the head*. Sheriff Watts was probably out of the picture maybe, for at least a couple of days. Anyway, Billy figured, the sheriff could have taken a bribe from Toms. So that left the gambler, Slam Beardsley. How could Wesley guess that Beardsley might want to tail him? Unless Beardsley was somewhere in the picture too. It all seemed like a game that Toms was enjoying.

But Billy gave up figuring at this point, and, by the time the moon had begun to slide away behind a stand of trees, the pain in his head had dulled so he was ready to drift off.

★ ★ ★

When he woke it was already light and Beardsley was stooped over a small fire, cooking up ham and eggs from the supplies they had got from old Bud Weaver. The food smelled so good that Billy rolled out of his bedroll and sat up immediately, and, despite the soreness in his head, he knew he felt a whole lot better.

'Thought you might like a bit of sustenance to fit you up for the chase,' Beardsley threw over his shoulder.

Billy poured water from his canteen over his face and went into the bushes to take a leak. He kept a wary eye out though he didn't expect to see the gunman he had chased creep back again. All the same, if a person had to be shot it might be more dignified to have his fly buttoned in place.

When he got back to the camp-fire and took the mug of steaming coffee Beardsley held out to him, he experienced a moment of contentment.

'It seems you have other skills apart from the cards,' he said.

'Surprising what you pick up along the trail,' Beardsley said. 'Are you somewhat restored to your normal self?' he asked sardonically.

'I'm OK to go on, if that's what you mean,' Billy said, putting the coffee to one side and starting to pitch into a slice of thick, fatty ham.

'Must have a skull like a rock,' Beardsley joked. 'You came back like Lazarus rising from the dead.'

Billy still had the bandage round his head but he jammed his Stetson close and tight so it wasn't too obvious. He chewed in silence for a while, thinking of what lay ahead and what the chances were of hunting down Toms and rescuing the two women. He gave

Beardsley a suspicious glance out of the corner of his eye and caught an amused look of enquiry in return.

'What?' the gambler said.

'What is this?' Billy said. 'There's something not quite on the level here and I aim to figure what it is.'

'That so?' Beardsley grinned. 'Tell Pappy what's on your mind.'

Billy chewed for a while in silence. The sun was getting up and everything came alive all round them. Birds hopped up and sang; a ground squirrel came out to look them over and pick up scraps from their breakfast.

'You rode into Sweetwater Creek; you spent a whole piece of the night gambling in the Bronco Saloon, then you took the stage to Laramie.'

'You got it right so far,' Beardsley said. 'Why don't you take a guess at the rest?'

Billy drained his coffee mug and turned it upside down. 'I figure this,' he ruminated slowly. 'You might be a whole lot more than you pretend to be.'

'More than a simple gambling man?' Beardsley gave him quizzical look. 'Tell me more.'

Billy shook the mug and held it out for more. As Beardsley poured coffee from the jug his hand was as steady as a rock.

Billy shook his head. 'Marshal Leavers was taking Toms to Laramie for trial. My guess is Toms was being taken in for what he did in Wyoming. But you and I know he had a record of robbery and killing down Colorado way. Right?'

Beardsley gave him a cool, shrewd look. 'Keep guessing, Billy.'

'My guess is you're wise about the Colorado business and the price on Toms's head down there.'

'You could be right there, Billy.' Beardsley gave him a look of wide appreciation. 'Those guys might have parted your hair but they didn't drill your grey matter. Why don't you proceed with your logical deductions.'

'Well,' Billy figured, 'It goes something like this. You've been trailing

Toms for quite some time, hoping to take him in and claim the price on his head. Somehow you got to hear that Leavers was taking him in and you guessed Toms would make some sort of escape attempt. Then you could run him down and claim the reward. In other words, you're a bounty hunter.'

Beardsley gave him such a close appraising look that the suspicion crossed Billy's mind that he might go for his gun. But that didn't make sense. Then Beardsley laughed.

'I put you down as a raw country boy, Billy, but now I see I was wrong. You got quite a head screwed on your shoulders and a deal of imagination to go with it. There was a big price on Toms's head down Denver way and I did think I might make a claim on it if I had the chance. Though taking Toms in was never going to be easy. Lucky thing Marshal Leaver caught him dead drunk. Or maybe it wasn't so lucky after all since Leaver is pushing up the daisies and Toms is still free.'

Billy grinned. 'You wouldn't have in mind to help him to escape yourself so you could take him in, would you?'

Beardsley threw up his hands. 'I may be a gambling man, Billy, but I only cheat at cards and with scum. I was just circling around waiting for something to happen in my favour . . . and it did. I could see how lax and careless Watts and Leavers were and I knew those bastards in the Toms outfiit would be waiting to come down and free that smooth-talking bastard. And' — he paused significantly — 'I knew that hard-faced waddy at the card table was one of Toms's men. I saw it by the way he looked you over.'

'How come?' Billy asked in surprise.

Beardsley touched the side of his nose. 'It isn't always what a man says; it's the way he acts. That's one advantage of being a gambling man: you learn how to smell out skunks and other vermin.'

Billy was still suspicious but he was satisfied. Beardsley had the sort of philosophy about life he appreciated.

'But I'll tell you something,' Beardsley added. 'That Toms is so slippery and so cunning, it's difficult to read his mind.'

'That's for sure,' Billy said.

Beardsley rubbed his stubbly chin thoughtfully. 'I got the weird impression he not only knows we're on his tail but he wants us to be. It gives him a thrill. It's all some kind of a game to him and when he wins and we're both dead meat he'll figure he's ace high.'

Billy nodded slowly. 'I figured the same thing,' he said. 'That's obviously why he left us a little reception party here by the river.'

'Right again.' Beardsley wiped his mouth on the back of his hand. 'So we got to move us carefully. We catch up with him, we hear him laughing, right?' He slapped his thigh. 'Tell you what, Billy: we catch him, we share the reward. Right?'

'Right!' Billy said.

13

They kicked out the fire, mounted up, and headed back to the river crossing where they had turned back the night before. They rode slightly apart in case the man who had crept in to steal the horses was still looking for trouble and was perched up there somewhere to take pot shots at them. Billy guessed that was unlikely since Slam had killed his partner, but you could never tell.

Down by the river they searched along the bank and soon found the tracks of Toms and his men again. There was a deal of tracks circling round the edge and on the bank on the other side.

Billy dismounted and looked at them close.

'Looks like they wanted us to think they crossed here,' he said, 'but my guess is they played the old river trick.'

'You mean they went back in and waded down a piece?' Slam Beardsley said. 'Seems possible. The river's quite shallow at this point.'

Billy was still examining the bush and the broken reeds along the bank. 'Sure. Look. This is where they went down into the river again.'

'Guess you're right, Billy. Those skunkbags want to shake us off their tails right enough. Toms must know you've got the hots for that piece of calico, Miss Nancy Partridge.' He gave Billy a broad suggestive wink. 'He's given you something to work out and he's enjoying this game, sure enough.'

Billy's face was as red as the sun through an evening haze but his voice betrayed no emotion. 'That Miss Nancy has a lot of courage. Since, in a manner of speaking, I was riding shotgun on that outfit, or should have been, I owe it to those two women to try to dig them out of this mess. And, by the way, I ain't got the hots for anybody!'

'Don't take offence, Billy. You know

what they say about a man who denies a thing too loud and too often.'

'I don't aim to ask!' Billy growled.

'But there's another thing,' Beardsley added. 'When Old Man Partridge knows his daughter's been kidnapped he's going to offer a big reward for her return. And Toms will count on that. If we nail Toms, that big reward could come to us. You know that?' He laughed and showed his gold tooth again.

'That doesn't make two bits of difference,' Billy said abruptly.

'OK, Billy. I was just kidding around,' Slam Beardsley laughed. 'Only question is, it looks like we lost the trail. So what do you suggest we do?'

Billy looked along the river towards the blue distant hills. 'What we do,' he said, 'is we ride along each bank, you on one side and me on the other, looking hard for the place where they rode out. A bunch of riders can't ride up the bank without disturbing things and leaving evidence, and it could be either side, I guess.'

Slam Beardsley frowned. 'Like picking through a haystack, Billy. But what if those tricky bastards doubled back instead of going on?'

Billy nodded. 'That's what I'm saying. That's why you ride along one bank and I ride the other. Savvy?'

Beardsley considered for a moment. 'Like tossing a coin, eh?'

'Could be,' Billy said, 'but I don't figure Toms would aim for the flat lands again. Too much chance of being tailed easy. More like he has some hideout up there towards the mountains. That's my guess.'

'OK, Billy. You're the boss till we come up against those ornery bastards.'

They rode on slowly, on either side of the bank, looking for sign. Billy wasn't too confident about Beardsley's ability to pick up the clues, so he kept to the left bank himself and let Beardsley take the right. The left bank was steeper and there were times when he had to veer away and return to the river.

The sun got up and it was hot, but,

as the sun rose, Billy's spirits declined. He knew there had to be some way of picking up on the outlaws' tracks, but he didn't have that much tracking skill, and the confidence he had shown at the crossing began to seep away. Maybe all that about the game was hogwash.

Then, looking across the river, he saw that Beardsley had stopped and pulled the Winchester across his saddle like he'd seen something suspicious. A second later Billy saw what it was: two figures riding along the opposite bank towards Beardsley. He pulled his horse in behind a stand of willows and steadied himself for a shot.

The two riders came to within 200 yards of Beardsley and drew rein. It looked like there might be a stand off. But Billy saw the two riders were Indians, Crow from the look of them. Both carried carbines in scabbards and the older man also had a bow and a sheath of arrows.

Billy eased his mount from behind the willows, held up his arm, and called out in his best Crow across the river. One of the Indians half turned to take a look and then raised his arm. Billy took his mount into the river and waded across until he was beside Beardsley.

'This could be tricky,' Beardsley said out of the corner of his mouth. 'You never know with Indians which way the cat will jump.'

'Could be,' Billy admitted. 'There again, it might be the Angel Gabriel in disguise.' He knew from experience quite a lot about the Indian nations.

He urged his mount forward until he was close enough to the Indians to speak. 'Peace to you, brothers.'

The Indians looked him over and nodded.

'Peace to you, Billy Bandro,' one of them said.

Billy tipped his hat back. 'Little Shoes!' he exclaimed.

The Indian gave a gruff chuckle. 'Good we meet, Billy,' he said, and then turned to his companion and said something in Crow Billy didn't catch.

Billy edged his mount a little further forward and the other Indian stared at him with hard suspicion. 'You friend Little Shoes?' he asked.

Billy nodded. 'We ride together sometimes. You headed for Red Rock Station?'

'We do trade,' Little Shoes informed him. 'Hear bad thing happen there.'

'News travels fast,' Billy said. He gave a brief account of the shootings at the outpost.'

'Bad medicine,' Little Shoes' *compadre* declared.

'This Yellow Wolf,' Little Shoes said.

Billy pointed at the scarf around the Indian's shoulder. 'Nice scarf you got there, Yellow Wolf.'

Yellow Wolf stiffened and the look of suspicion returned.

Little Shoes muttered something reassuring and showed his teeth. 'Yellow Wolf find this thing on bush close to river way back there.'

He turned and waved his hand up-river.

134

Beardsley had drawn in beside Billy. 'What's this about?' he said.

'This is a little gift from the angels,' Billy said. 'That scarf Yellow Wolf is wearing belongs to Nancy Partridge. I saw her wearing it back in Freshwater when she got on the stage.'

He remembered she had been wearing it when he saw her on the balcony of the hotel the night before they left Freshwater Creek. He remembered the way she had smiled at him and her friendly greeting, and once again, he knew he had an obligation to do everything he could to save her from Toms and his bunch. When he saw Yellow Wolf with the scarf draped proudly over his shoulders it made him feel unaccountably determined.

As though he felt the flame of Billy's anger, Yellow Wolf put his hand up to the scarf and gripped it. Before Billy could speak again, Slam Beardsley intervened. He explained to the two Crow men in a mixture of sign language and English how Miss Nancy

Partridge had been wearing the scarf when Toms and his gang had carried her and her aunt off after the shooting at Red Rock.

The two Indians listened with interest and increasing dismay before engaging in an animated discussion in their own language.

'You think they're telling the truth about the kerchief?' Beardsley muttered quietly to Billy.

'I'd place bets on it,' Billy said.

Little Shoes nodded and turned to Billy. 'Yellow Wolf agree. We show you were we find this thing on bush. Yellow Wolf good man reading sign. He show you.'

The two Crow wheeled their horses. Slam Beardsley turned to Billy and raised his eyebrows. 'Looks like we got lucky.'

'Like I told you, the angel came,' Billy said.

Billy and Slam Beardsley urged their horses on in the wake of the two Indians.

14

When they reached the bend in the river, it was obvious. Though the waters were deep on their side there were shallows on the other shore, and this was where the outlaws had scrambled out.

They urged their mounts into the faster flowing waters and drove them across. When they were on the other bank, Yellow Wolf took off the silk scarf from his neck and draped it with some delicacy over a broken branch. This was where the whole bunch had climbed up on to the bank and ridden off in the direction of the mountains.

And another thing to note: as Billy looked at the silk scarf hanging from the branch, he imagined how it had been and how Nancy Partridge had casually and skilfully left the scarf trailing so that whoever might follow could pick up the trail.

'Like you said,' Slam Beardsley said, 'that young woman has guts. We have to go on and find her.' His voice sounded more humane and more determined than Billy could have believed.

He thought, it's one thing to want to follow and another thing to do it. It had been his practice to set a course by the stars or track bear and mule deer by their claw or hoof prints. Keeping on the trail of a bunch of killers intent on hiding their tracks was another thing entirely.

'We thank you for helping us,' he announced formally to Little Shoes.

Little Shoes nodded phlegmatically.

Billy speculated on what he could give these two unexpected angels to thank them for handing them the clue they needed. When he looked up he saw that Yellow Wolf was staring at Slam Beardsley and, in particular, at the gold watch-chain hanging from his tooled vest.

Yet Little Shoes showed no interest in

this. Instead, he swung off his Indian pony and went bobbing and bending up the trail to where it disappeared among stunted trees. A moment later he returned and gestured towards the trees.

'They go that way. We follow there.' He pointed a stabbing finger in the direction the outlaws must have taken.

Yellow Wolf wrenched his eyes away from Slam Beardsley's gold chain and grinned. 'We follow there.' He pointed up the trail towards the trees.

'You know what,' Slam Beardsley said in surprise to Billy, 'these guys mean to go all the way.'

Billy nodded. Nothing surprised him about his Indian friends. A little time earlier when Little Shoes had an arrow in his arm, Billy had cut it out and sucked the poison from the arm and bound up the wound. It wasn't so much that Little Shoes owed him, but that the simple act of mercy had forged a kind of kinship between them that could never be broken. He said nothing of

139

this to Beardsley, but simply turned in the saddle and grinned.

'Trust me, Slam. These guys intend to help us any way they can.'

'You mean they don't have business of their own to attend to?'

'Oh, yes, they have business, but they also have the loyalty of friendship. That's a lesson you have to learn, Slam, and you might get to take Toms in and claim your bounty reward after all and even get something from Nancy Partridge's pa.'

'Is that the truth?' Beardsley crowed, but with acid in his voice. Now they were on the trail, maybe the reward seemed a little less important.

* * *

They cut along at quite a remarkable pace, the two Crow riding ahead and scouting the trail which was clear in places and less clear in others. They paused briefly towards sundown to snatch a bite of jerky and to gulp water from their canteens, but the excitement of the trail was flaring in Yellow Wolf's blood and he gave them no rest.

'We ride on,' Little Shoes explained. 'May be it rain soon and wash out trail.'

Billy had peered at the sky several times as they rode along and, though he saw no sign of rain or storm, he respected the Indians' decision.

When the sun had hidden itself behind a stand of trees ahead, Yellow Wolf raised his hand and called a halt. He led them to a stony bluff and straight to a cave, and it was clear he knew the lie of this country as well as he knew his friends.

'We rest here,' he said. 'Sun-up we ride on. Find those bastards and free the women. OK?' His suddenly cheerful voice raised Billy and Slam Beardsley's hopes as they hobbled the horses and settled down in the cave. Little Shoes took charge of the domestic arrangements. He drew a blanket across the narrow entrance to the cave and lit a small fire where they could cook and brew up their Arbuckle's. The two Indians were well-supplied with jerky and pemmican and even chuck wagon chicken. Somewhere high above there were cracks and fissures that served as chimneys. So the smoke from the fire was by no means suffocating.

Slam Beardsley started fumbling in his saddle-bag for the bottle of rye he always carried, but Billy put a restraining hand on his arm. 'Don't even think about it,' he whispered as the chuck wagon chicken sizzled on the fire. 'Drink coffee and be satisfied.'

Slam Beardsley raised his eyes to heaven but accepted Billy's verdict. He had forgotten that Indians reacted badly to gut juice; if Yellow Wolf took more than a couple of sips he might become a different and far less amenable man entirely.

Yellow Wolf had, in fact, been watching Slam Beardsley's movements with keen interest but, when Billy handed him a mug of Arbuckle's, he guzzled it down and seemed well satisfied.

Little Shoes drew the blanket aside and went out to see to the needs of the horses. An Indian always knew how to look after his horse which was his lifeline and his strength.

When he returned he squatted on his haunches and looked at Billy with concern.

'Maybe the rain come over the mountains tomorrow. We ride first light. Gain ground on those badmen. OK?'

Billy and Slam Beardsley said it was OK and the four men spread their bedrolls and settled to sleep.

Though Billy was weary, his head had ceased to throb from the bullet that had grazed his skull. He thought briefly of Toms and the crooked way the man thought, and wondered what the next day would bring forth.

15

At first Billy thought he was dreaming. Then he thought they were under attack with the wild whoops and roarings that rang through the cave.

The fire had died down to embers, but there was enough light seeping in from outside to see the forms of his companions, one of them leaping and dancing like a crazy man! It was Yellow Wolf, the old Indian, and Billy realized immediately what had happened. After watching Slam Beardsley reach into his saddle-bag for his bottle of rye, the Crow had waited until they were all asleep. Then he'd reached in himself, uncorked the bottle, and swigged back rye like it was lemonade. Now he was waving the empty bottle like a war club and prancing around like he might bring it down on any head within reach.

Slam Beardsley had drawn back to

the side of the cave and was fumbling to release his revolver as Little Shoes struggled to get a grip on Yellow Wolf and bring him down.

Billy reached across and gripped Beardsley's wrist. 'Don't get that sixer out! And for God's sake don't start blasting around in here!'

But Beardsley was too mad afraid to listen. He shook Billy off and hurled him aside. As he went for his gun again Billy came in low and brought him down. Beardsley was no pigmy-sized *hombre*, but Billy was big and strong and he quickly pinned him down among the rocks where the cave slanted up to the roof.

Little Shoes and Yellow Wolf were still struggling for supremacy on the other side of what remained of the fire. As they grappled with one another Yellow Wolf rolled on to the ashes. He bellowed and thrust upwards, hurling Little Shoes back against the wall of the cave. Little Shoes sank down against the rock and capsized like a sinking ship.

Roaring and hooting, Yellow Wolf retrieved the bottle and smashed it against the rock. He turned and made as if to lunge at Billy with the broken bottle. But Billy had managed to free himself from the tangle of Beardsley's limbs and, as the Indian blundered in, he took a swing and caught him on the side of the jaw. Yellow Wolf staggered back and fell, sprawling among the debris by the fire.

'Stay there!' Billy warned, as Slam Beardsley blundered to his feet and felt for his gun again.

Billy went to Little Shoes and raised him gently into a sitting position with his back to the cave wall. 'You OK?' he muttered. He could hear Little Shoes' quick breathing and guessed he would soon revive. So he splashed water from his canteen on to his face and Little Shoes grunted and pulled himself up, muttering something in Crow.

'It was the fire water,' Billy said. 'Yellow Wolf grabbed the bottle and drank the lot.'

'Yellow Wolf like crazy man with fire water,' Little Shoes growled.

Billy went to the fire and heaped up what was left of the dead wood they had gathered before settling down for the night and soon the fire revived and the cave began to be cosy and warm again.

While the others gathered their thoughts, or pulled themselves back into the world of relative sanity, he brewed up more Arbuckle's and handed it round in their tin mugs.

The swing to Yellow Wolf's jaw had laid him out real cold and the rye had at last poleaxed his spirits. So now, apart from a few twitches and groans, he lay peaceful as a babe.

Slam Beardsley came and stooped over him. 'I thought he was going to kill us all, the son of a bitch.'

'You gotta remember,' Billy warned, 'Indians react differently from us to alcohol. It gets to them real quick. I don't know why; it's just a fact. You should have kept that bottle hidden completely. When that poor guy nosed it out, he couldn't resist the temptation. So now you've got nothing to drink but pure spring water.'

'Pure nothing,' Slam Beardsley said, squatting morosely by the fire to consider matters. 'So now what do we do come sun-up?'

Billy squatted beside him and looked across at Little Shoes who had also drawn up to the fire and was looking decidedly glum.

'I guess we do what's necessary,' Billy said. In the small hours of the morning their chances of doing anything other than giving up the chase seemed remote.

'What do we do, Little Shoes?' he said.

Little Shoes slowly raised his head in the flickering light of the fire. 'Like you said, Billy, we do what we have to do.'

★   ★   ★

Once again they settled into sleep but it was a restless sleep in which they dreamed Yellow Wolf would creep up on them before dawn and slit their throats. Slam Beardsley, the gambling man, was less trusting of the native people than Billy. So for the next two hours, he kept his hand on his gun and one eye open and glanced frequently across at the still sleeping form of Yellow Wolf.

After the tussle, Billy soon plunged into the deep chasm of sleep. Years on the trail had trained his body to sleep as soon as his head hit the pillow or touched the rock where he happened to lie, but he was equally quick to wake as soon as something stirred in the camp.

When he woke again it was to the faint rustle of air as Little Shoes yanked back the blanket and looked out at the faint pre-dawn light.

He got up and started immediately to rustle up breakfast: beans and more prairie chicken, and, even more essentially, mugs brimming with Arbuckle's coffee.

'Decision time!' he shouted, and Slam Beardsley jerked awake from his fitful and none-too restful sleep.

Little Shoes came in and squatted by the fire. Billy thought he looked a trifle more optimistic as he handed him his mug.

They chewed and drank for a while in silence and outside the sky began to grow pale with the light of dawn.

Little Shoes rose from the fire and went to inspect Yellow Wolf who lay on his back, his breath bubbling through his lips like an old engine hard put to keep puffing. 'Yellow Wolf have very big bad head,' he announced and nobody denied it.

'What do we do?' Slam Beardsley asked.

Little Shoes gave him a straight and open look. 'We go on,' he announced. 'We track badman and then . . . ' He made a decisive gesture which might have indicated a knife being drawn across a man's throat.

'What about Yellow Wolf?' Beardsley asked.

Little Shoes glanced sceptically at the

slumbering form lying against the bend in the cave. 'Yellow Wolf stay. Sleep off bad drink. No good now.' He made a slow contemptuous gesture of finality. 'We pick up Yellow Wolf after we track badman and save woman. OK?'

Slam Beardsley gave a slow sigh of relief. 'That suits me,' he said.

16

They left Yellow Wolf lying like a curled up wolf or bear facing the wall of the cave. He had what he needed to eat and drink when he came too sufficiently, and Little Shoes had made sure his pony had enough freedom to graze and drink from a spring close by.

'Suppose a bear comes, or a pack of coyotes. What does he do then?' Slam Beardsley asked solicitously.

'No bear is going to come into a cave that smells of man and whiskey,' Billy assured him. 'When Yellow Wolf comes to, he'll have a very sore head. He'll lie around moaning and pitying himself for a while. Then he'll either go back the way we came and blame Little Shoes for letting him make a fool of himself, or he'll follow on and try to catch up on us.'

They set out briskly with the dawn

rising over their right shoulders and the birds starting to twitter and crow all round them in the treetops. It might have been a picture of Eden except for the bank of greyish cloud drawing up like a dirty blanket over the hills ahead.

'It's going to be a washout,' Beardsley declared pessimistically and Billy knew he was right. If a big storm swept down from the hills it could be enough to wipe out all traces of Toms and his men, even for a scout like Little Shoes or Yellow Wolf.

But so far Little Shoes seemed undeterred and he rode on with confidence towards the gathering storm.

When the rain came at midday it struck the ground like curtain rods, so that almost at once the whole landscape was draped in a furious hissing cloud. Billy pulled his Stetson down over his eyes and urged his horse on through turbulence and rain that lashed their faces like whips. It lasted for half an hour and, when they came through, Little Shoes was still riding, though he no longer seemed to be reading the signs on the trail. After another hour they came to what was left of a ruined cabin and pulled in under what was left of a canopy.

Billy dismounted and nosed his Remington in through what remained of a door while Little Shoes hustled the horses into a dilapidated barn and began to dry them off with handfuls of straw and musty hay. Indians knew that caring for your horse was always ace high when you were on the trail.

Inside the gloomy cabin nature had almost taken over control again. Creeper and plants of all kind had invaded through the walls, but there was a table leaning heavily against what was left of a wall. Billy stooped and peered into an ancient stove. Then he ran his hand over the top and found it faintly warm.

Someone stayed here last night, he concluded.

Slam Beardsley appeared in the doorway. The storm had taken its toll. Though he still wore his gambler's outfit, he was looking kind of dilapidated like life had pulled him down a piece. He grinned and leaned against a sagging wall.

'So, this is where the story ends,' he declared. 'I always knew the Devil had the last throw.'

'Not so quick, Slam,' Billy said. He was picking around among various items on what was left of the table: a broken pipe, a stray bean dropped by a greedy man. 'Someone's been here in the last few hours. You can smell them in the air.'

Slam Beardsley sniffed like an old hound but apparently smelled nothing but mould and decay.

Little Shoes appeared in the entrance looking like he'd caught a big fish with a small pin. 'They stay here last night,' he announced. 'Toms and badmen rest up here.'

'How d'you know that?' Beardsley demanded. He couldn't believe that the Indian had led them through that storm to exactly the right place.

Little Shoes grinned knowingly. 'Track marks under roof. One bent hoof. Same one we follow. They stay here.' He nodded confidently.

'How did you know?' Beardsley asked him.

Little Shoes touched his nose. 'Me savvy. Know this place. Old Man of the Woods live here. Good place to stay.'

Beardsley looked round in dismay. Compared even to the cave they had occupied the night before, this was fetid and gross. He couldn't believe anyone would ever want to rest here.

But Billy was occupied on his knees close to the ancient stove. There, crumpled among dead leaves and filth on the broken floor, was a small silk handkerchief. He picked it up and carried it to his nose and caught the faint scent. It was the same scent he had caught from Nancy Partridge when he helped her on to the stage before the stage pulled out of Freshwater.

'Little Shoes is right.' He straightened up. 'That woman has enough balls and enough wits for two men. She figures we'll be right behind them.'

Slam Beardsley took the handkerchief from him and held it to his nose. 'You're right, Billy. She dropped this for us to find.'

Billy took the handkerchief and tucked it into the pocket of his vest.

Little Shoes was also inspecting the cabin. He placed his hand on the stove and grunted. He moved around the room, stooping, glancing this way and that, reading the signs.

'Bad night,' he said at last 'These badmen have bottle too. Fight plenty. Tie women to post here.'

'How does he know that?' Slam Beardsley asked in amazement.

Billy was looking at the signs too: an abandoned piece of rawhide; the marks of friction on a post propping up the roof; a broken bottle with bloodstains on a jagged edge.

'Little Shoes is right,' he said solemnly. He didn't want to say what he'd seen. Nancy Partridge and her aunt had made a play for freedom; they had been tied to the post. Toms and his men had fought and blood had been shed. Billy didn't like to think any further. He wanted to get to the horses and ride on immediately.

But Little Shoes had other ideas. The horses must rest and eat. An hour lost would be two hours gained on the trail.

'There's some sense in that,' Slam Beardsley conceded. He rolled a quirly and sat on an old bench letting himself be drenched in the sun. Little Shoes squatted beside him and Beardsley rolled another quirly for him.

Billy prowled back and forth under the drooping canopy and stared out among the trees. The handkerchief had revived his hopes and aroused his fury against Toms and his brutal *compañeros*. A desperate need urged him on to finish the job he had set his mind on doing no matter what it cost.

17

When Little Shoes figured the horses had rested enough they held a council of war.

'Which way now?' Billy asked Little Shoes. His own modest woodcraft skills caused him to doubt whether they could make any further headway against Toms and his bunch.

Little Shoes went sniffing around the tracks round the ruined cabin. To Slam and Billy the confusion of hoofmarks was a puzzle too hard to read, but Little Shoes turned his face in every direction and sniffed the air as though some clue about Toms and his men might still be drifting on the wind.

'We go this way,' he said. Then he swung on to the back of his pony and set off through the trees to an area of scattered chaparral and occasional cactus.

Billy and Slam Beardsley stared at

one another in astonishment. Then they shrugged their shoulders and followed, watching Little Shoes as he paused from time to time to assess a broken branch or a deeper hoofmark.

Presently he stopped and gazed at the hills that loomed closer. The storm front had passed and a scattering of less formidable clouds was scrambling over the peaks.

'What do you think?' Billy asked him.

Little Shoes knit his brow and considered deeply. 'Think I savvy,' he said solemnly.

'Savvy what?' Slam Beardsley said.

'Savvy where badmen headed,' Little Shoes affirmed.

Slam Beardsley surveyed the wide country with a sceptical grin. 'That's a tall order,' he said quietly to Billy. 'How can that savvy be more than a hunch?'

Billy gave him a quizzical look. 'I'd place more bets on Little Shoes and his hunches than all your sneaky card tricks shuffled together. He knows this wilderness a whole lot better than we do. It's kind of ancestral. And instinct too. I guess he's thinking of a good place where you could hole up for months if you didn't want to be seen or heard.'

'There must be plenty such places in this wild country,' Beardsley marvelled.

But as they mused, Little Shoes held up his hand and they froze instinctively. They could hear the pounding of hoofs coming towards them across the open country.

Without stopping to talk, they urged their horses into a little dip behind a stand of low spruce.

The riders soon came in sight, as many as fifteen bobbing figures moving steadily through the bush. Little Shoes peered out through the spruces. 'Shoshone!' he pronounced with contempt.

Now Billy could see the riders outlined quite clearly. He saw they were Indians but wouldn't have been able to distinguish the tribe. He wasn't surprised by the Crow's response. Though the Crow and Shoshone tolerated one another, they didn't speak the same language and there wasn't a whole lot of love lost between them.

'A woman!' Little Shoes exclaimed, just as Billy saw for himself. Amidst the Indian riders there was the gaunt, frail form of a woman. You could tell by the stiff jerky way she rode that, though she was no stranger to horses, she was old and somewhat stiff in the shanks.

'What the hell!' Beardsley exclaimed. 'I'll be damned! That's no squaw woman! Looks like those red men have taken her prisoner.' He urged his horse out into the open and levelled the Winchester at the advancing riders.

'Pull back, Slam!' Billy said. 'What in hell d'you think you're doing?'

It was too late. The Shoshone men came to a sudden standstill. Billy heard them jabbering together in a sudden panic. And then they wheeled and with warlike whoops began to discharge their weapons. Bullets and musket balls flew like angry hornets all round them.

Beardsley levelled his weapon but, before he could fire, his horse started to buck and kick up its legs, and he very near pitched back into the hollow.

'What the hell!' he roared, struggling to bring his spooked horse under control.

The Shoshone kept firing somewhat randomly in their direction. But one of them, who looked like he had the manner and authority of a chief, steadied his horse and lined up for a better shot. Before he could fire, Little Shoes called out in broken Shoshone and waved his arms above the parapet.

There was another round of wild shouting before the Shoshone calmed down. Billy heard the chief giving his orders in a gruff tone of authority. Then everything quietened except for the shrill cry of the woman nagging to be saved.

For a moment Billy had thought and hoped against all the evidence it might be Nancy Partridge; now he realized that the woman riding among the Shoshone was her gaunt-faced Aunt Emily.

'Back off with your gun, Slam!' he said. 'This is the time for *parlez vous* not shoot at you.' He held up his arm and rode up from the shelter of the hollow to meet the Shoshone braves. As he rode forward slowly, he was aware of Little Shoes on his right shoulder.

Little Shoes went forward and he and the Shoshone chief parleyed for a moment in Indian sign language. Billy knew that sign language had limitations. So parleying might be tricky.

As the two Indians tried to make themselves understood, Emily Partridge kept up a hysterical wail from among the ranks of Shoshone braves who stolidly ignored her.

'Mr Bandro!' she cried. 'You are Mr Bandro, aren't you? Why don't you save me from these heathen men?'

'Rest quiet, Miss Partridge,' he promised. 'That's just what we mean to do.'

The Shoshone chief gave him a shrewd glance. 'You know this woman?' he said in clear English.

'Sure I know her, Chief.' Billy urged

his mount closer to the thief, a man of middle years with a barrel chest and a keen aquiline face. 'You speak good English.'

'My father was a big man, kinsman of Washakie, friend of the Americanos. He learned to speak good English.'

Billy knew about Washakie, the Shoshone peacemaker. He smiled: 'Your father must have been a great counsellor for peace. But why is this Americano woman riding among you?'

A quick look of concern passed over the chief's face. 'She's no prisoner though she screams like one. We found this Americano woman wandering and groaning way back there. She told us the bad Americanos had left her to die. So we saved her though she doesn't believe it. We brought her along with us.' He looked about him with pride. 'So now we give her to you.'

The chief made an abrupt signal and several Shoshone braves helped Emily Partridge down from her horse and brought her forward. What a strangely changed Miss Partridge it was. No longer the rather stately and proud sister of the biggest rancher in Laramie district, more like a fluttering bird with a broken wing. Her long and stylish dress, totally unsuitable for riding at the best of times, was just a bundle of torn rags smeared with black stains and ash.

'Those danged varmints left me to die,' she complained.

'Don't worry, Miss Partridge,' Billy said. 'You're going to be OK. You must thank the chief for saving your life. You could have died out there with no one to help you.' Billy wasn't used to offering words of comfort, so they came a little awkwardly on his tongue. But the Shoshone chief grinned and the braves nodded approvingly.

'Now we make camp and eat,' the chief proclaimed.

The whole company gathered in a hollow where there was shelter from the now hot sun and one of the Shoshone braves began to beat on a drum of celebration.

Billy couldn't keep his mind on these necessary rejoicings. Seeing the bedraggled state of Miss Emily Partridge, he was too concerned for the safety of her niece, Miss Nancy Partridge.

CENTRAL WEST LIBRARIES

18

Slam Beardsley must have experienced a rare moment of true gallantry.

'Miss Emily!' he said. 'You're looking in prime condition, though, if I may say so, your dress looks a little frayed.'

Emily Partridge immediately burst into tears and covered her face with her hands. 'It's been terrible, terrible,' she sobbed. 'Those awful men and that horrible animal Toms!'

The Indians stared at her in stolid amazement. Tradition had taught them the code of pain and hardship: when the going gets rough you clamp your teeth together and get on with life the best way you can. And their women were stoical even in childbirth.

Slam Beardsley was already on his feet rummaging in the saddle-bag he'd managed to rescue after the shooting at Red Rock Station. 'Listen here, Miss

Emily,' he said with rough compassion 'I've got a few things you might consider throwing on. A mite more suitable for the trail than what you're wearing.'

Miss Emily stopped sobbing and looked up. After a second her lined, pale face creased in a smile. 'Why, thank you, Mr Beardsley. That's really gallant of you,' she croaked.

The Indians stared at Slam Beardsley in amazement and a kind of strawberry flush appeared on his face. 'The clothes are nothing to sing about, Miss Emily.' He held up a check shirt and a pair of faded jeans, 'But I guess you might be more comfortable in them on the trail.' It probably didn't occur to him that he looked out of place with his gambler's duds on, not to mention his big knuckle rings.

Emily Partridge seemed more than pleased with his offer and she disappeared under some bushes at the other end of the hollow and soon she was sitting on a withered tree-stump dressed in the mannish clothes and devouring jerky with the rest of them. Sitting next to her, Slam Beardsley seemed suddenly like the Big Bad Wolf after he had been tamed.

'I hardly like to mention this, Miss Emily, but how bad did those desperadoes treat you?' he asked.

The sudden thought of Toms and his bunch made her eyes dart with panic and she almost screamed again. But she fought for control and growled out, 'Those men are real cruel! They behave like wild beasts!'

'No need to upset yourself, ma'am,' Billy said. 'You're safe now with us.'

'But,' she cried, 'I had to leave Nancy and I felt like I'd been sold into slavery when these Indians came along.'

'Except these Shoshone men came along just right to rescue you, Miss Emily,' Billy said. 'Can you tell us how that came about and' — he paused — 'what exactly happened to your niece Nancy?'

Emily Partridge stared into the distance and then her face hardened.

'Oh, my God! What am I thinking about! Yes, here I am going on about myself when I should be thinking only of Nancy. Poor Nancy! Those wicked men are still holding her. What are we going to do?' She looked from Billy to Slam Beardsley in dismay.

Slam Beardsley patted her arm in a fatherly way. 'Don't fret overmuch,' he said. 'Billy and I aim to rescue your niece and make sure you both get safely home to Laramie.'

Little Shoes muttered in approval and the Shoshone braves growled in response.

'If you can bring yourself to it,' Billy said, 'why don't you tell us exactly what happened?'

The gaunt woman glanced around her, saw the Shoshone chief's look of encouragement, and told her story.

* * *

It seemed that when they reached the ruined cabin, arguments had already

171

broken out between Toms's henchmen. There was a fight between the man with the hickory-hard face Jeremiah Dandy, who was no dandy, and another member of the gang who had been slashed with a bottle. Toms had intervened and somebody had bound up the man's wrist to stop the flow of blood. Nancy and her aunt had complained so vigorously that Toms had had them tied to the post with rawhide. That accounted for the blood-stains on the post.

At sunup they had ridden on and the two women had complained so bitterly and employed so many delaying tactics that Toms had decided to cut Emily loose and leave her on the trail, probably to die.

'But he kept my dear Nancy because he wanted a reward!' Emily wailed. 'I don't know what's going to happen to that poor girl!'

Lucky, the Shoshone band had arrived and the chief decided to take mercy on Miss Emily and carry her along with them.

'Apart from the tying up did they treat Miss Nancy really bad?' Billy asked.

Emily had got beyond complaining now. She simply nodded dumbly and set her jaw. 'That man Toms, he pretends to be awful nice, but he's a bully and a brute. I think he means to keep Nancy for himself and still blackmail my brother Ralph into paying a lot for her release.'

Billy considered for a moment. His imagination conjured up a picture of Toms the bully and Nancy Partridge, the girl he remembered smiling down at him from the balcony of the Grand Hotel in Freshwater Creek. Something inside his stomach turned over and he winced.

'What are we going to do?' Miss Emily asked.

Billy looked her over and wondered how the hell they would manage to go and track Toms and his sidekicks with this grumbling old harridan in tow.

'What we're going to do, Miss Emily,'

Slam Beardsley piped up, 'is follow those ornery bastards and shoot hell out of them. That's what we're going to do.' His voice sounded so strong and determined that Emily Partridge gasped with admiration. 'I believe you will, Mr Beardsley. I believe you will. And I'm going to ride along with you and make sure we win through and free that girl!'

Billy considered for a while. How the hell could they free Miss Nancy Partridge with that woman hanging round their necks like a rock tied to a man in a river?

'Did you get any clue about where they're headed, Miss Emily?' he asked her.

She knit her brows. 'I don't think so, Mr Bandro. There was a lot of talking and arguing and abusive language but nobody spoke of their destination.' She shook her head. Her eyes widened. 'But there is one thing I do remember. That hard man, the one who hit the other with a broken bottle, he said he was looking forward to lying down before the king.'

'Lying down before the king,' Billy repeated in amazement. Though he couldn't make it out, he felt it should somehow be an important clue. 'Who's the king?' he muttered.

'The king,' said Slam Beardsley, 'he's the guy they have in England. Only now I hear they got themselves a queen. The king's the guy in charge. Some people call him the monarch.'

'That's right, Slam,' Billy said.

'I know King!' Little Shoes said suddenly. 'That's Big King, rocky place. Is up there in mountain.'

'Yeah,' Billy said thoughtfully. 'Come to mention it, I heard tell of Big King.' Sure he'd heard of Big King. Old Jake Jacks had mentioned it a few times as they rode together on the stage.

'That's where Toms and his outfit are heading,' Little Shoes announced with unexpected certainty and enthusiasm.

Billy and Slam Beardsley turned to look at him. 'By God you're right!' Billy said.

Little Shoes nodded solemnly. 'Big King. That's where we follow.'

★   ★   ★

Billy wanted to get on to the trail immediately, but there was such a thing as protocol and they had to bide a while and parley with the Shoshone. The chief wanted a full account of the shoot out at Red Rock Station where he traded frequently. Billy told him about Eldridge Toms and how he was wanted by the law down Colorado way as well as in the Wyoming territory — though he didn't mention the price on Toms's head. He knew the chief had a lot of savvy and could make at least five out of two and two. And he knew enough to avoid offering to join the party headed for Big King.

The chief had been studying Slam Beardsley closely with his cool shrewd eyes and Billy could see he wanted to get his fingers on Slam's much-coveted watch.

Slam saw it too. He drew a silver chain out of his vest pocket and dangled it in front of the chief. At the end of it swung a wrinkled silver pig. 'Here, Chief, take this as a mark of thanks for rescuing Miss Emily here,' he said.

The chief's eyes gleamed momentarily. 'That's good.' He popped the chain and the pig into a little medicine bag on his belt and stood up. 'We have much to do,' he said. 'Too much to ride to Big King right now. Bad place. Many spirits of many dead people. You rescue the woman and kill Toms. Make things better and we'll be happy.'

He raised his hand and all the Shoshone braves got to their feet.

'We go as friends,' he said.

'We go as friends,' Slam Beardsley agreed solemnly.

The Shoshone mounted their horses and within two minutes they had ridden off to the south, leaving the small party alone to consider their next move.

19

'What do we do with Miss Emily?' Slam Beardsley muttered quietly, when they were mounted up.

'Nothing we can do but take her along with us,' Billy replied. He knew Slam Beardsley had a point. A woman on the trail in a time of war can be a hell of a liability.

Slam screwed up his face, and then grinned. 'What happens when the shooting starts?'

Billy had considered that too. 'I guess we have to tell her to hold back out of the line of fire.'

Beardsley showed his gold tooth again. 'I can't abide a woman's screaming. It puts me off my aim.'

Billy grinned. 'Then you better plug up your ears with that old calico dress of hers. Unless you want to cut her loose again so she can take her chance with the coyotes and the timber wolves.'

'That's enough of that whispering about me,' Emily Partridge said suddenly in a loud and strident tone. 'I may be an unmarried old maid, but my hearing's pretty sharp and I can handle a gun as good as any man. You think I spent most of my days in the wilderness for nothing?'

The two men swung round to look at her and both were struck by the same thought She looked kinda homey in the men's clothes Slam Beardsley had lent her. They made her look a deal younger and more chirpy. Billy figured she couldn't be much more than forty, and now that the immediate danger was passed her face had brightened up more than a tad! And she had a flinty determined look in her eye.

Slam Beardsley touched the brim of his hat. 'Beg pardon, ma'am. We were thinking of your safety, that was all.'

'We just want what's best for you, ma'am,' Billy added.

'You want for me not to scream and

holler?' she said. 'Well, OK. I won't scream and holler. I don't scream and I don't holler when there's work to be done. My main work now is to rescue my niece Nancy. So give me a gun to shoot with and I'll shoot those murdering men down as good as any man.'

'I believe you would, Miss Emily,' Billy said. 'But best you stay in the background, and leave the shooting to Slam and me and Little Shoes here.'

'You just give me that gun and I'll shoot every one of those beasts,' she emphasized with spirit.

Billy had been considering the best approach to the mountain. Though he had never been to the rock some called Big King and others called the Monarch he knew it would be tricky. It wasn't just a rock: it was a high fertile plateau cradled among rocks. Like a big double molar with food in the cavity. A man standing on the highest rock called Indian Lookout could see any coming danger as easily as a knight looking out from a high tower in an old castle.

Billy glanced at Little Shoes. 'You know the layout around King Rock, Little Shoes?'

'I know it good,' Little Shoes boasted. 'My people know. Many years my people go there and spread tepee.'

'Is there a way up there without being seen on the way?'

Little Shoes wrinkled his brow. 'I know ways. We try.'

But before Little Shoes could enlarge on the subject, their attention was drawn to a rider approaching quickly from the left at their rear. Slam Beardsley grabbed his Winchester and swung to face the oncoming rider but, before he could raise the Winchester, Little Shoes had dashed it down with his hand.

'Yellow Wolf!' he cried. 'Brother Yellow Wolf!'

The rider drew to a halt and raised his hand, and then trotted towards them. It was Yellow Wolf, for sure. He sat high in the saddle with no hint of embarrassment or a hangover. When he drew close enough, Billy saw that he looked refreshed and fine as though he had been on some sort of rest cure.

'Yellow Wolf,' he said. 'We greet you!'

'I greet you!' Yellow Wolf replied like an old warrior returning from many campaigns.

He and Little Shoes engaged immediately in a excited babble in Crow.

'What does he say?' Slam Beardsley demanded.

Little Shoes pulled his face into a frown. 'Not good,' he announced.

'Why not good?' Slam Beardsley said.

'Yellow Wolf thinks we go back to Red Rock Station,' Little Shoes said solemnly.

An expression of anger and dismay crossed Slam Beardsley's face. 'What for? I don't aim to go back anywhere until we've seen this thing through,' he rasped.

'What about that poor girl?' Emily Partridge whined. 'We can't leave her in the hands of those beasts.'

Billy looked profoundly thoughtful

for a moment. 'Why does Yellow Wolf want to go back to Red Rock Station?' he asked.

Little Shoes and Yellow Wolf conferred again briefly. Little Shoes tilted his head. 'No more surprise,' he said. 'Yellow Wolf picked up trail. Someone trail us here. Know we head for hideout at Big King. Means Toms and outfit will wait, shoot us like jack-rabbit or prairie chicken.'

Billy stroked his chin and considered. 'I guess that must be the man who tried to steal the horses back there, the one who got away. He must have been on our tail ever since. Maybe we should have tracked him down and shot him before we crossed the river.'

'We should have dropped him cold like that other bastard,' Slam Beardsley said.

'There can be no never mind about that now,' Billy said. 'We've got to decide what we do.' He turned in his saddle and looked at Little Shoes. 'Yellow Wolf might be right at that.

Maybe you and Yellow Wolf should go back. If we go on we all risk being shot down before we reach those bags of — ' He glanced at Emily Partridge and buttoned his lip.

'So you won't go on and rescue that girl?' Emily Partridge squealed in dismay.

'I didn't say that, ma'am,' Billy said. 'I aim to go on whatever. I'm just saying these two Crow braves should go back if they want to. They've done a great job anyways tracking those outlaws No need for them to risk their lives for a cause they have no stake in.'

'Another thing,' Slam Beardsley said. 'Now we know where those guys are holed up, we could go back to Freshwater and rustle up a posse. Come at them with force. That would be the common-sense way.'

Billy stiffened. 'I don't think we can do that. I don't trust that ornery sheriff Watts anyway. I'm not sure he wasn't half hoping Toms might escape. I have a hunch about that and I could be wrong.

And he hates our guts after we humbled him so much at the station.'

'That's what I want to hear you say,' Slam Beardsley agreed. 'I'm all for going in. I never did a good thing in my life before now and it's about time I started.'

Little Shoes raised himself in his rawhide stirrups and held his hand firmly against his chest. 'Me go to Big King!' he said. 'Time bastard men smoked out!'

Yellow Wolf nodded gravely. 'We smoke 'em out. But I have hunch too. Like Yellow Wolf say, the man who track us. He go ahead Big King and warn Toms and his bunch we come.'

'Then we have to slide in some other way,' Billy said.

'Is there any other way?' Slam Beardsley asked.

For a moment nobody spoke. Then Yellow Wolf piped up solemnly. 'There is other way. It difficult and slow. We go there. I show you plenty.'

20

Billy felt like a general without an army. By his calculations there must be at least eight in Toms's outfit, maybe as many as ten. Ten seasoned gunfighters against two gringos, two Crow Indians, and a possibly hysterical woman who might shoot off every which way and possibly wound or kill men on her own side. And Toms had the additional advantage of the best position and the knowledge that Billy and his bunch were on their way. It would be a damn fool thing to go on and he knew it.

Yet maybe things weren't quite as bad as they seemed. Billy had the two Crow Indians and Big King was a place they claimed to know from ancestral times. Could he trust them? he wondered.

Little Shoes chose a good camping place for the night, sheltered but high so that anyone approaching would need to climb up and probably betray himself with a fall of scree. This time they made a cold camp which was very uncomfortable specially when the temperature dropped right down. They took turns keeping watch except for Emily Partridge who wanted to insist on taking her place on watch until Slam Beardsley convinced her it was a job for a man and more especially for a Crow Indian. Then, after a frugal supper since stores were getting low and there was no fire, she settled down in a soft place Slam had found in the shelter of a rock and apparently fell into a sound sleep with her hand close to a Winchester they had lent her to humour her. A little too close for Billy and Slam's liking.

While Yellow Wolf stood guard on a high rock, the other three gathered round and Little Shoes sketched the layout of Big King with a stick on the sand. It was like an irregular horseshoe with a single way into the valley where they assumed Toms and his men had their hideaway.

'They know we're on our way. So how do we play this hand?' Billy mused. 'And does Yellow Wolf really know another way up?'

'We could just ride in like hell and blaze away,' Beardsley said.

'And get ourselves killed immediately!' Billy reasoned. 'I don't think that's going to help Nancy Partridge none. And it sure ain't going to help our skins.' He pondered for a moment. 'You know I once heard of an English guy. His name was Wolfe, I think. You know how he tricked the French? Place called Quebec in Canada.'

Slam Beardsley considered himself an educated man but he had to admit the only Wolf he'd heard off was the timber wolf that he sometimes heard howling at night in the hills.

Billy grinned in the faint light from the stars. 'Wolfe and his soldier boys climbed a big precipice and took the French off guard. That's how they beat the Frenchmen and captured the city.'

Slam Beardsley stared at him with

suspicion. 'Is that right? Could we do that up at Big King, you think?'

Both men turned to Little Shoes and Little Shoes shook his head. He had only partly understood the story of General Wolfe. So Billy explained again with reference to the stick and the marks in the sand. Little Shoes stared at the scratchings for a long time and then called out to Yellow Wolf.

Yellow Wolf left his post and scrambled down to confer with Little Shoes.

'Trail's here,' Yellow Wolf said, tracing a way round and between the bluffs with the stick.

'Could we climb up there?' Slam Beardsley asked.

'Big climb,' Little Shoes said dubiously. 'No horse climb up there.' He raised his hand and held it vertically. 'Steep. Big steep climb.'

'But it can be done?' Billy suggested hopefully.

Little Shoes paused to consider. 'Steep and . . . ' He wriggled his hand.

'Steep and windy,' Billy said. 'And

narrow,' he added.

'And plenty dangerous,' Slam Beardsley added. He was brave with a gun and competent on horseback but climbing rocks had never been part of his agenda. 'What happens if we fall?'

Little Shoes grinned and brought his right fist down hard on the palm of his left hand. 'We fall,' he said. 'We fall like tumbling rocks and we get to the bottom like' — he looked around for a comparison and found none — 'like dead meat,' he concluded.

The men sat in silence for a while, each picturing his own descent from the rocks. Shivering from the cold was one thing; shivering from the fear of rolling down those cliff-like heights was something else again.

'That's the way we have to do it,' Billy concluded.

Yellow Wolf explained he knew the way up and had climbed it several times when he was a young man counting coup. They could do it from the south side from where there was a dense forest of junipers where they could leave the horses. It would mean starting before dawn and riding in a wide semi-circle almost to the foot of the rocks.

'What about Miss Emily?' Billy said.

Slam said, 'We have to leave her with the horses. It's the only way.'

'I don't aim to be left with no horses,' Emily piped up. They thought she was still asleep, but she had taken in the whole conversation. 'If you're gonna climb, I climb,' she added.

Billy felt sort of uneasy about that but he didn't see any other solution. So he agreed and they slept, taking turns to keep watch and, some time before dawn, Billy roused himself and crept round, prodding the others awake. The Indians woke immediately and seemed to be as fresh as butter. Slam sat up swearing and fisting his eyes. And Miss Emily struck out with her fist and caught Billy just below the eye. When she realized where she was and what she had done, she apologized. 'I thought those desperate men had crept into the camp,' she said. 'Now what do we aim to do?'

Billy gave her a mug of cold water and outlined the plan. 'We ride as soon as we've had our chuck,' he said. 'If you won't stay with the horses down there as you insist, then you'll have to climb along with us.'

'Just as long as I get to keep the Winchester,' she said.

Billy shook his head. 'We don't have too many guns to spare, Miss Emily. If we're going to rescue your niece we're going to need all the fire-power we have . . . and in the right hands too.'

'I told you I can shoot as well and straight as any man,' she insisted. 'If I stay down in that forest with the horses I might be attacked by wolves or a bear,' she said. 'Then I shall need all the fire power I've got, too. So I'm coming with you anyway.'

Billy saw that they had no alternative but having her along on the climb. She was lean and she had muscles, but would her nerves stand up to the fight? He had to believe it!

From the way she looked at him he concluded she had a deal more courage than he had previously figured.

★   ★   ★

They rode out cautiously before the first rays of the sun began to tip the hills and hit the prairie. They took a long sweep round to the south as Little Shoes led them towards the little craggy mountain that made up the Big King. Well before they got within spitting distance of it, they saw it rising above the juniper forest with a kind of red raw majesty that filled them with creepy unease.

Nobody could climb those sheer cliffs, Billy thought. Yet he had come to trust Little Shoes and knew that when the Crow Indian said he could do something, he did it.

By the time they reached close enough to the foot of the rocks to tether the horses the sun was already high enough to paint the tops a dappled orange though the juniper forest was still deep in purple.

'You think we been seen yet?' Slam asked.

'I hope as hell not,' Billy said. Since they had been riding through thickets and stunted trees for two hours or more it seemed unlikely that anyone had spotted them.

They rode on through deep stands of juniper until Yellow Wolf led them into an open glade where there was good grazing for the horses.

He held up his hand. 'We stop here,' he said in a quiet voice.

Billy and Slam looked up at the side of Big King. It might not be much of a mountain as mountains go, but they could see its steep sides and knew that if a man or woman fell there wouldn't be much to stop them before they reached dead bottom . . . or reached bottom dead!

'My, that's gonna be some climb!' Miss Emily Partridge said. And she was right!

21

The going was tough, much tougher even than Billy had anticipated and certainly much tougher than a gambler like Slam Beardsley might have expected. Billy could see that as Slam Beardsley peered up what seemed to be a sheer cliff to where dark birds of prey circled in the blue above. But the Crow Indians seemed to have the knack of climbing, especially Little Shoes. After conferring briefly about the best route up and where were the most likely handholds, Yellow Wolf paid out a lariat they had carried along with them. Little Shoes hung it from his waistband, turned to the others and pressed his index finger to his lips. 'We keep very no speaking,' he muttered.

The others nodded in agreement. Every sound here would echo and ricochet off the rocks and into the forest. It would be like asking to have burning black pitch poured down on them from above as in an ancient castle.

'Maybe we should have just gone in there like I said,' Slam Beardsley grumbled to himself.

'Well, we're here,' Billy said, 'and this is the way it's going to be.'

Little Shoes reached for the best handholds and, when he felt secure, he hoisted himself up. At first he seemed hesitant, but, as soon as he was established, he swarmed up like some kind of monkey and it was clear that many years before he had practised scaling these very rocks. When he was twenty or thirty feet above he secured his rope to a projecting rock and signalled to the others to follow. Billy went ahead to set a good example though he felt decidedly shaky in the knees. The perch where Little Shoes had established himself was a little ledge no more than a foot wide — scarcely enough for a wild crow to rest on.

'Can we do this?' he muttered, when he was up there with Little Shoes.

'We do it,' Little Shoes whispered between his teeth. 'Going gets better up there.'

Now came Miss Emily. Yellow Wolf tied her to the end of the rope and they hauled her up. She was quite light and when she lost her grip and swung out from the rock they held her suspended like a spider or more of a dead fly and hauled her up on to the ledge. Though she kept a grim brave face and managed to stifle her screams Billy felt her trembling beside him on the ledge.

Now it was time for Slam to come up. Billy had seen how nervous he was because he had seen the whites of his eyes and noticed how hard and quick his breath came before the climb. Slam was no lightweight either. So holding him on the rope wouldn't be easy, especially with the narrowness of the ledge. Slam was obviously no climber so they eased him up little by little on the end of the rope. Though he paused every so often to gasp and take a breath, he kept himself against the rocks and gradually improved his climbing technique. When he was with them on the ledge, he hung on to the small pinnacle where the rope was attached so that, if he fell, he could hoist himself back up again.

Then came Yellow Wolf and, like Little Shoes, he swarmed up the rock face like a monkey, though a somewhat older and greyer monkey.

Weapons were hauled up and they hung suspended by another rope.

Yellow Wolf had spurned the rope and now, without a pause, he went on for the next pitch which was almost as difficult as the first, though there was a slightly better ledge to rest on up there. Soon they were roosting up there like a bunch of somewhat bedraggled crows. The drop now seem so long they tried to keep their eyes from looking.

'Easier now,' Little Shoes promised. Maybe he was just saying it to keep their spirits up.

Yet it did get easier. They crossed by a difficult and narrow traverse and found a winding path worn by mountain goats. Though it was no picnic trek, after the almost sheer precipice it seemed like heaven. So they climbed on between projecting rocks and the occasional bushy outgrowth. Now that the going was easier they turned their thoughts to what might lie ahead: the possibility of who knew what when they reached the top of the ridge. Though they tried to climb in silence, an occasional slither of rocks made what Billy thought was one hell of a noise. Each time they hugged the rock and waited for signs of life from above. Then they would move on as cautiously and silently as stalking cougars, inch by inch to the top.

It seemed a century before they crawled on to flat stone and flopped down like salamanders side by side on the top of the sun-warmed rock. Billy raised his head cautiously above the edge and saw a valley opening up below. It looked like the promised land he had read about in the Bible one time. He had only half believed that Toms and his bunch were holed up in such a heaven of a place until he saw smoke curling up and then the roof of a cabin below. It was crude but enough to bide awhile and live and had probably been built by an old-timer way back and then abandoned. It had a roof of logs covered with dry grass to form a thatch. A string of horses was hitched to a rail close by. He could even hear music, or what passed for music, as someone blew on a mouth organ inside.

'Kind of homey, ain't it?' he whispered to Miss Emily.

'Homey nothing,' she growled, hoarse as a man.

Billy raised his head a little higher to take a better look at the layout. Slam Beardsley, having recovered some of his courage and self-esteem, began to pass the weapons along. Miss Emily grabbed her Winchester possessively and immediately checked its action. That seemed a good and determined thing to do.

Billy held up his hand. He had heard something or someone moving close to his left and, as if by a conjuring trick, the head of a man in a grey floppy hat appeared leaning on a projection of rock and staring down towards the valley entrance — the lookout man. If they had done what Slam Beardsley had proposed and approached in a cloud of dust all guns blazing, they'd have been seen coming for miles.

The lookout man turned almost directly towards them and peered over the edge of the cliff. Something below had caught his attention: a fall of rock perhaps; the distant neighing of one of the horses. Or maybe he had heard their earlier sounds and wanted to check whether it was a mountain goat. His face in profile was tense and alert and he held his gun close, ready for use. Obviously they were expected.

Billy signed to the others to keep their heads down. The two Indians and Miss Emily ducked but Slam Beardsley was checking his Winchester and there was the scrape of metal against rock. Yellow Wolf reached out to stop him but it was enough.

The man on lookout swung towards them and Billy saw red-rimmed eyes bulging with amazement and fear. The man opened his mouth to yell but the yell never came. Instead came the pulpy thud of Little Shoes' knife striking his chest. The man reached up to claw at the hilt spurting crimson and then wheeled and rolled. With a crash of foliage and falling scree he disappeared over the side of the cliff towards the valley and the peaceful-looking cabin.

A horse below reared and whinnied. A man ran out of the hut, shaded his eyes, and stared up in their direction.

'You up there, Bart? Where the hell you hiding yourself?'

Then he saw something beyond their view: the body of the lookout man sprawling halfway down the bluff with a knife sticking out of his chest, shirt stained blood red, and eyes wide with the horror of his own death.

'Oh, my Gawd!' the man bawled. He turned and disappeared behind the cabin.

After two seconds all hell broke loose. The man reappeared and took three quick shots at the ridge way off to their right.

'Keep your heads down!' Billy warned. 'And spread along the ridge!' He knew they had the advantage and it would take a few moments for the men below to figure exactly where they were.

Slam Beardsley eased the Winchester forward and pumped in two returning shots. The man below spun round and blundered back among the horses. The horses reared and plunged as men spilled from the cabin, some tugging at their jeans, others with their coats half on, half off.

'Like shooting clay pigeons!' Slam Beardsley shouted, as he gave the outlaws blast after blast from his Winchester.

It was almost the last thing he said.

Another man appeared below. Billy had just a moment to recognize him as Jeremiah Dandy.

'Get your head down!' he said to Slam Beardsley. But it was too late: Jeremiah Dandy took a quick bead on Slam and a bullet smashed into Slam's face and sent him spinning and spurting blood.

'Oh, my God, they hit him!' Emily cried. She scrambled, monkey-like, down the ridge where the fallen man lay face up to the sun.

There were no goodbyes, or you've been my best buddy. Slam's dead! Billy thought. Beardsley was dead before he knew he'd been hit. And the man who had hit him was the hickory-faced bastard with the tooled saddle who had tailed them from Freshwater Creek to Red Rock Station — the bastard who had probably put a crease on Billy's skull. He was some shootist!

'Slam's dead!' Miss Emily cried from below. 'They killed him!'

Billy couldn't grieve. There was no

time for grief. He had had a growing respect for the gambling man and had never quite figured why he had wanted to come along with him. But now Slam was dead and the time for grieving would come later.

Billy took stock of their position. Two Indians and a woman in deep shock. A woman who might now be a burden to them all.

But those two Indians knew their business. Both had crawled away to seek better cover. Billy lay exposed on their left and the man with the face of a carved image was taking a bead on him too. As he ducked down behind a rock a shower of rock and dust spurted up where his head had been. There was a roar and another man reared up on his left like a giant sprung from the ground with a Colt in each hand, spurting flame alternately. His bullets whined like angry hornets as they clipped the rocks and spun away . . . too close, far too close. Billy caught the smell of cordite as he rolled for cover and struggled to bring his Remington into play. Damn! he thought. We had every advantage and we threw it away!

'You yellowed-gilled bastard!' the hickory-faced man shouted from below.

Billy raised the Remington and pulled the trigger on the man with the two Colts. But there was only a click! The Remington had jammed! He threw back his arm and hurled full into the advancing ugly face. And it missed! Yet it was enough to spoil his aim. As the man came blundering on Billy scooped up handfuls of dry sand and threw them into his face.

Then he lunged forward, head low, hoping hickory face couldn't pick him out from below and be too furious to care. As he lunged forward a huge disappointment broke in his mind. This should have been easy! This should have been a cinch! Like shooting clay pigeons, as Slam Beardsley had said with almost his last breath.

His head struck the man just below the heart. The man's breath gasped out and he fell back. Billy dropped on to him and for an instant they struggled together and Billy caught the stench of rancid breath and stale tobacco. The next moment they were rolling and bumping together among sharp rocks and what seemed like the longest descent in history! The man had his claw-like fingers deep into Billy's neck. So he was scarcely aware of the thud of rock and gravel against him as they rolled together halfway down the bluff.

Almost to the bottom! In a spasm of reflex action Billy hurled the man off and lay struggling to retrieve his breath. Hickory face was still there somewhere trying to get a bead on him. Crawling towards the man with the Colts, Billy tried to drop down on him again and pin him to the ground but, despite the stink of alcohol and tobacco the man was in no mean condition. Hard and lean, he reared over Billy and dropped down on him. Billy curled and rolled. He knew in his gut that when the bulk of the man hit him he would be crushed flat as a beetle and finished. With all his remaining strength, he slithered to one side and kicked up in an instinctive stomach throw and connected. He caught a last glimpse of the face, hideous with pain and streaked with blood as the man rolled over him arc-like and disappeared into a hollow below.

Billy lay helpless on his back for what seemed like a generation, a generation when the world appeared to fall away and recede and nothing was of any account any more. Then he felt the sting of splintered rock on his back and heard the high whine of bullets striking close and knew hickory face was still trying to get a bead on him.

22

He felt and looked like a blood-soaked bundle of rags, but rage and adrenalin surged through his system. It shouldn't have happened like this! He should be winning this fight against Wesley Toms and his bunch of no-good desperadoes!

He rolled over and crawled for cover. He wiped the blood from his eyes and reached for the Remington that wasn't there. He could see a little below a wild mêlée of horses and men milling around, trying to hoist themselves into the saddle, turning to fire past him on to the ridge. Others were firing from the cover of the cabin.

Some comfort came from the firing from behind him and above. Little Shoes and Yellow Wolf had obviously stayed calm and taken advantage of their position. Three of the Toms bunch lay sprawling dead or wounded in the area around the cabin. But there were others, maybe as many as half a dozen returning the Indians' fire. And there might be more inside the cabin. Not to mention their prisoner Nancy Partridge! Though Billy trusted Little Shoes, he knew from past experience that, when their blood was up, Indians could fight like demons from hell!

I've got to take decisive action here, he thought, struggling on to his knees and looking for some way to crawl or run. A bullet snicked his shoulder and he ducked again! Maybe one of the big man's shooters was still around though it didn't seem likely. He could see the bulk of the man lying perfectly motionless on his back but the two Colt revolvers had bounced away and could lie anywhere.

Where was hickory face now? he wondered.

As Billy peered round, ducking whenever one of the desperadoes aimed a shot at him, he heard a high cry from above and Little Shoes came sliding towards him into a bush. For a moment Billy thought Little Shoes had been hit. He started to crawl towards him, but the Indian stuck his head out from behind the bush and shouted, 'Here, Billy! Take Winchester!'

The Winchester '73 that Slam Beardsley had carried ever since the shooting at Red Rock Station came sliding down the slope towards him . . . and stopped, it must have been ten feet away, wedged against a rock. If he crawled out to retrieve it, the man shooting at him from below could drill him twice before he reached it. At the same moment Little Shoes, crouching behind the bush, began to pump slugs with deadly accuracy at the men below. A man staggered and ducked and disappeared behind the cabin. Billy half swam, half crawled to grab the Winchester. He turned and wriggled into position so he could pump one off as soon as the man showed his face again.

And still, where was hickory face and, more to the point, where was

Wesley Toms and Nancy Partridge, for God's sake?

Then something he wasn't expecting happened. He heard a sound between a whine and twang and a flaming arrow arced through the sky above him and struck the roof of the cabin. Then another zinged down and embedded itself between the grass and dry logs. Then came a third, whizzing past and striking a lean-to packed with hay. The roof was tinder dry and in five seconds, flames began to shoot up from the roof of the cabin and from the lean-to.

What the hell's that crazy Indian think he's doing? Billy thought. Nancy Partridge is inside there. They'll come out cooked as roast turkeys!

They did run out of the cabin. There must have been half a dozen at least. Quite a bunch! They came coughing and retching and staggering to reach their horses. The flames leapt like the flames of hell and a great billowing of smoke began to swirl from the roof of the building.

Yellow Wolf was pumping his arms up and down and shrieking a blood-thirsty war cry in which Little Shoes joined enthusiastically.

But where is Nancy Partridge? Billy thought.

'Where's my niece!' Emily hollered from above. 'That poor girl must be in there somewhere!'

A sudden thought spelled out in Billy's mind. He must get down to the cabin somehow and get that gal out of there before she was hurt. Without thinking about the possible conse-quences, he grabbed the Winchester and hurled himself down towards the cabin. Damn hickory face and damn Toms. I got to pull that girl free before the smoke or the flames kill her! He ran and he slithered and he fell and struggled to his feet again until he was only feet from the cabin. Now shooting with any accuracy was difficult or impossible because of the billowing fog of smoke and everything struggling in confusion. The horses were going mad with terror. Through the haze he saw men struggling to free their horses and ride away from the turmoil.

Billy stooped to retrieve a revolver from a dead man. Better than a Winchester at close quarters. He checked to see that five chambers were loaded and stuck it through his belt. He would need every last bullet.

He turned to find Little Shoes crouching beside him. Through the smoke they could see men and horses wheeling like phantoms. He heard Yellow Wolf and Emily Partridge still firing above though the targets were blurred. Every second or two they changed position which gave the impression there was a whole bunch up there. My God, that woman's got grit, he thought.

'I'm going in!' he said to Little Shoes. 'I've got to get that girl out! Whatever happens I've got to get her out of there.'

Little Shoes nodded vigorously and shouted up at Yellow Wolf. Yellow Wolf stopped firing and Billy assumed he would give him cover as he fought his way into the cabin. He edged forward and then ran, knowing Little Shoes would guard his back.

'Nancy! Nancy Partridge!' he shouted.

There was no reply. My God she'll be roasted alive, he thought as he kicked at the door. The door swung open and he was confronted by a man with a shotgun. 'Get out of my way!' the man bellowed. He swung the shotgun round, but, before he could fire, Billy discharged the Colt into his chest. The man leaped back, the shotgun blew in a deadly plume at the ceiling and he fell with one leg dancing in the air.

'Nancy! Nancy Partridge!' Billy shouted again, but there was no response. Now the room was almost full of choking smoke from the burning roof.

'Not there!' Little Shoes shouted.

Billy pulled away from the door. 'Where is she?'

'She ride off!' Little Shoes gestured through the smoke.

'What d'you mean — rode off?' Billy said savagely.

Little Shoes pointed to his own eyes. 'I see. She ride with man. That way!'

It was clear: Toms had made a break for it, taking Nancy with him, probably on the same horse.

'I'm going after them!' Billy shouted. 'I have to go after them!'

But at that moment, the wheeling badmen had decided to group for a counter-attack. He heard them and saw them coming in closer through the smoke.

He knelt and pumped lead at them as they came charging and wheeling round him. Five shots and three men down. A man was riding close, prancing and firing. Billy saw the streaks of flame from the man's shooter and felt the hot acrid breath on his cheek.

Ain't so easy to hit a man from a prancing horse, he thought, as he lunged forward and made a grab at leather chaps and yanked. The man, wide-eyed with fury and panic almost fell on top of him, but Billy pistol whipped him and he rolled away to be

216

chopped down by Little Shoes.

Little Shoes sprang to the horse's neck and twisted it round.

Before he could reason or think, Billy had swung into the saddle and grasped the reins.

'I'm going after that bastard Toms!' he yelled.

'I cover for you, Billy!' Little Shoes shouted.

23

One thing to say he was going after Toms and Nancy Partridge; another thing entirely to do it. Right at that moment Billy felt so high on adrenalin he could have flown up into the sky like an eagle and looked down over the land and the hills and the mountains and picked Toms out as he rode with Nancy Partridge like small miniature figures across the landscape. He didn't give a damn whether he was hit or not. He was invincible! Some ancient god was ready to shield him.

He just rode out through the smoke ignoring the forms of the riders shooting at him through the haze. He didn't return their fire because he had invisible armour and he figured it was a waste of bullets and, anyway, Yellow Wolf and Little Shoes could do enough damage from where they were. So he rode in the fury of a madman from hell out through the smoke and the haze to where it was clear. And that's when he was surprised.

Yellow Wolf had inflicted crippling damage on the Toms bunch with his withering and accurate fire from the Winchester '73. It was like he had saved all the resentment and humiliation of his nation's suffering and channelled it into one big blast. The desperadoes were in total disarray and those who hadn't been wounded or killed were riding to put as much distance as they could between them and what they supposed was a whole tribe of Indians on the warpath.

Yet Billy couldn't feel any pleasure. Despite his vision about being an eagle riding high above the land and looking down to pick out those pygmy forms, he had to admit he had no notion where Toms and Nancy Partridge were. If Toms had ridden off with Nancy shielded by the smoke — that was assuming he had been in the cabin in the first place — he had no clue about which direction he might have taken.

So he wheeled round, calmed himself down and tried to take stock of the situation. While he was considering, Little Shoes drew rein beside him. He had picked out a stray horse in the corral and looked ready to face anything.

'Little Shoes ready,' he declared. 'What we do?'

Billy put his hand up to shade his eyes. The sun was now quite high and burning down on the land.

'We try to figure which way they ride,' Billy said between his teeth.

'Only one way out, and only one way in,' Little Shoes told him. 'We ride out and circle till we pick up trail.'

Billy nodded curtly. With those riders riding away from the cabin down into the approaches, picking out Toms's horse would be something close to a miracle.

As they considered, two forms approached through the haze. Yellow

Wolf and Miss Emily Partridge. They had also managed to find loose horses — broken-down nags from the look of them.

'They ran away!' Miss Emily shrieked. 'Those bastards hightailed it like the rats they are.'

Well, Miss Emily is still fully functional, Billy thought. Slam Beardsley's death had done nothing to weaken her resolve. If anything, it had strengthened it.

'We smoke them out,' Yellow Wolf said, showing his teeth with obvious delight.

'Trouble is,' Billy said. 'We don't know whether Toms was in that cabin, not to mention Miss Nancy. It might be Toms lit out before we got here. Knowing we were on our way an' all.'

'That figures,' Miss Emily said, 'but I think you're wrong about that.' She spoke with such conviction that Billy gave her a sharp look and wondered whether she had an inner eye that told her things beyond ordinary comprehension.

Little Shoes was nodding as though he shared this uncommon vision of the world. 'We go on, find 'em,' he pronounced solemnly.

So they rode on down the defile that led up from the arid plain to the comparative fruitfulness of the place where the burning cabin stood. As they picked their way down, the two Indians read the sign though this was difficult since maybe half-a-dozen riders had passed that way, trying to get clear of Yellow Wolf's withering fire from above.

I've been a fool, Billy thought: a real damned fool! Slam was right or at least half right. Instead of scaling that dizzy cliff face, he should have positioned himself down here somewhere so he could pick off the fleeing riders as they rode down from the cabin. Anyway, now he's gone so that don't figure.

When they reached the lower region, the two Indians parted and started looking for sign. Their work was made a little easier since they could still pick out the distant forms of fleeing riders.

After a time during which Billy had champed his jaws continuously and Miss Emily's eyes had darted about furiously over the landscape, Yellow Wolf held up his hand and pointed to the right. 'Toms go that way,' he declared confidently.

'Are you sure about that?' Billy asked.

'Sure,' Yellow Wolf nodded. 'Up there along Snake Pass. Only way get through. Look. Two horses go this way.'

Billy leaned forward and studied the sign. Sure enough the hoofmarks of two horses had branched off to the right in the direction of Snake Pass instead of taking the way down that would lead them back in the direction of Sweetwater. Toms had probably gone for Snake Pass. It made good sense. But who was the other rider? The face of the man with hickory face who had followed them and then killed Slam Beardsley swam into his mind. Jeremiah Dandy, he thought. That haunting figure who had winged him and put an end to Slam Beardsley's gambling days.

'Two riders,' Miss Emily said recklessly, 'one of them carrying away my sweet Nancy.'

'And one of them the man who killed Slam Beardsley,' Billy muttered.

Miss Emily bit her lip and straightened her back. 'Then that's the way we must ride. I've got to rescue that poor girl and avenge that poor good man's death.'

Billy glanced at Little Shoes. 'Better if you bided here, Miss Emily. Let us go ahead. We can ride a lot faster even on these broken-down nags. Why don't you go back and bring the other horses. We might need them at that.'

A look of shock and dismay followed by disgust passed over Miss Emily's face. 'Why do you ask me? I can ride like any man. And I wouldn't stay here on my own anyway. What if those desperate men decide to turn and ride back. I couldn't shoot them all on my own, you know.'

Billy nodded. He knew there was no restraining this virago woman. Yet they might need those horses they had left hobbled in the woods the precipice. It could be a long ride before they caught up with Toms and Dandy and a string of fresh horses might make all the difference.

'OK,' she said. 'I see these nags might not be quite fit. They look a little saggy in the jaws and droopy in the eyes.' Her eyes darted over the two Indians. 'Why don't we ask these two good men to go back for the horses?'

Little Shoes and Yellow Wolf exchanged angry growls. They were both fired up and neither would relish the thought of missing any action that might take place.

After a moment of silence Yellow Wolf piped up, 'I go for horses. Not take long. I follow like the wind in the trees. We catch those bastard men and we kill them.'

Miss Emily nodded grimly. 'In that case we don't have much time to waste,' she declared. 'I suggest we ride on and trust to Little Shoes' good judgement on the trail.'

Billy was still doubtful about the arrangement. Yellow Wolf had proved himself a valuable asset in cleaning out that desperate bunch around the cabin with his Winchester. But, like she said, there was no time to waste. So he agreed.

★   ★   ★

Billy and Miss Emily and Little Shoes rode on up the defile that led to Snake Pass. Though Billy hadn't been that way before he soon began to see how the pass had got its name. It was a snake in form as well as name, winding to and fro up the mountain side. Narrow and winding and taxing for both horses and men.

'You know this pass?' he asked Little Shoes.

Little Shoes grinned. 'Since long time. My people and other Indian people ride here many times. It go over other side. Hard riding. Good that Yellow Wolf follow with fresh horses.'

Yet, despite loose rocks and stones, Little Shoes kept looking for sign and spotting it. He stopped a moment and reached down and plucked a piece of dark material off a cactus plant. 'Here!' he announced with a smile. 'Miss Nancy skirt. They pass here.' That meant at least that Nancy Partridge was with Toms.

Billy insisted on riding second along the narrow defile, following close behind Little Shoes. Miss Emily kept up on his horse's heels. That old girl is a real stayer, he thought, as she urged her nag hard to keep up with him.

The way was not only winding and hard going for the horses, he could see that ahead it narrowed even further with steep inclines on both sides. A good place to stage a bushwhacking, he thought, peering up to right and left through the dazzling sunlight.

They rode for a long time before

Little Shoes held up his hand and called a halt.

'Why are we stopping?' Miss Emily cried. 'We got to keep after those varmints.'

'To spare the horses,' Billy said. 'They're already blown. And look here, there's a little water-hole. They must be thirsty as hell.'

They dismounted and let the horses drink, though Billy could sense Miss Emily's agitation from the way she muttered to herself. Yet when he scooped up water in his hat, she took a long drink. The water was far from fresh and could give them the gripes to say the least, but they were almost as thirsty as the horses, so nobody complained.

Yet there was little time to rest and Billy hugged his carbine, searching along the surrounding rocks for a glint of steel. He still had that uncomfortable feeling they were riding into a trap. Anywhere along this trail they could be like sitting ducks in a shooting-gallery.

Little Shoes was mounting up again. Billy put out his hand to help Miss Emily into the saddle, but she brushed it off with a swing of her arm and swung up easy on her own, though he noticed she groaned a little.

At first the way ahead was no easier than it had been before. The pass narrowed so they could ride only single file along the path with high cliffs rising on either side. They kept as quiet as possible because every whisper seemed to echo into a scream in this high country. Up above predatory birds circled and cried over the cliffs, craning their necks and searching the rocks below for carrion or prey.

Then the high cliffs drew back and the pass opened up and nature seemed to spread and sigh with relief. But not for long.

It suddenly happened, but not as Billy had expected. As a small rock-strewn glade opened out before them, Little Shoes suddenly drew his mount to a halt and slid off its back. Billy followed suit like a lizard slipping from a rock. He caught Miss Emily by the leg and hauled her down from her mount. Though she glared at him she picked up his danger signals and followed through.

'Look ahead!' Little Shoes croaked.

Billy looked past Little Shoes and immediately saw what he had seen — the body of a woman tied to a rock, head hanging down.

'My God!' Miss Emily shrieked. 'That's Nancy! What have they done to that poor girl.'

24

The woman hung like a scarecrow from the rock she was tied to. She could have been alive, or she could have been dead. The clothes she wore were torn and tattered. Billy remembered the moment when he had helped Miss Nancy Partridge on to the stage, the smile she gave him, the waft of her perfume and the way she had waved her silk scarf from the window. He recalled seeing her on the balcony of the Grand Hotel and the brief conversation they had had. And he grimaced at the thought of her hanging humiliated and broken on that rock.

'My God, they killed her!' Miss Emily shrieked. 'They killed that dear sweet Nancy!' Her voice was enough the startle the buzzards circling above and to alert anyone crouching behind the rocks to their presence.

'I don't think she's dead, Miss Emily,' Billy said.

As if to confirm his suspicion, the girl raised her head slightly and then slumped forward again, her knees crumpling and sagging, head drooping on to her chest.

'She moved her head!' Emily said. 'That dear girl is alive!'

'She's alive,' Billy agreed, though he could see that she might be closer to death than to life.

Miss Emily sprang forward impulsively. 'I've got to get to her!'

Billy caught her in a grip like an iron clamp. 'Hold back, Miss Emily!'

'But don't you see, she needs me? I must get to her. She's right out there in the sun and she's been hurt real bad. That poor girl is dying!'

'You can't go to her, not yet.' Billy tightened his grip.

'But why? She needs me!' Miss Emily pleaded. Billy felt her arm fighting to free itself but he held on.

'You go out there,' he said quietly,

'you're asking to be shot down. You know why they put her there tied to that rock? They put her there to use her as bait. You go out there, that's what they want. They'll kill you, Miss Emily.'

'But I've got to do something to save her,' Emily cried. 'If I don't do something she's gonna die anyway.'

Billy could see what she meant. The poor girl was in a very bad condition and, though the cliffs on either side were steep and high, the sun was already glaring down on the frail form. Soon Miss Nancy would be burning like a lost soul in the torments of Hell.

Little Shoes was peering over his horse's back, scanning the tops to right and left and watching for any sign that would give away the position of Toms or Dandy. At a guess, Billy thought, those two skunks will have taken up positions on each side of the pass to catch us as we move in to take the bait.

Miss Emily had stopped struggling. 'What are we going to do?' she wailed.

Billy caught Little Shoes' eye and

nodded. 'What we do, Miss Emily, is I go out there and cut your niece loose.'

A look of astonishment came into her eyes. 'You can't do that. They'll kill you for sure.'

'They'll try,' he conceded. 'That's why they put her out there.'

'If I go they might not shoot,' she said. 'Don't you think they might take pity on a woman, Mr Bandro?'

Though he didn't show it, Billy laughed inside. 'Makes no difference to a man like Toms. Man or woman makes no difference,' he said. 'Those men are killers. They show no pity except to themselves when they're being killed like rats fleeing from a burning barn.' He turned to Little Shoes. 'Brother Little Shoes,' he said quietly, 'I'm going out to get that girl. You give me cover?'

Little Shoes nodded grimly. 'Up there,' he said, indicating the ridge to their right?. 'I see moving.'

'Sure and up here to the left,' Billy said.

'I'll cover your left.' Miss Emily

moved into position with her Winchester.

Billy tried to work out the range and thought the weapon might throw a shell to the top of the ridge and wound or kill a man. Or it might not. Anyway, he had to take a chance and, with Miss Emily throwing to the left and Little Shoes throwing to the right, he had a chance of maybe one in three of making it to the rock and cutting Miss Nancy loose.

Then he had another idea. 'I'm going to count to three and go, and I'm taking these horses with me.'

But before he could begin to count a voice came from the rocks above, somewhere to the left. 'Hi there, Billy boy,' it said, in a weird echoing voice that ricocheted off the cliffs all round the pass.

Miss Emily and Little Shoes and Billy drew back instinctively. Billy surveyed the ridge to their left.

'That's Toms,' he said. 'So I guess Dandy must be up there to the right.'

'You coming out to meet me, boy?' the voice of Toms crowed out again eerily. 'Maybe we could make a deal on this.'

'Keep looking,' Billy said quietly. He reckoned Dandy, who he knew was a deadly shot, would be up there to the right somewhere. That was where the chief danger would come from.

'Are you listening?' the voice of Toms echoed around again.

'I hear you,' Billy said. 'What deal had you in mind?'

A laugh bounced among the rocks. 'The deal is this,' Toms said. 'That young woman is feeling and looking kinda low. She wants someone to untie her from that hard rock so you can nurse her and take her back to Freshwater. I know you always had a soft heart, Billy.'

'So what's the deal?' Billy shouted.

'Well, you're a man of honour, Billy,' the voice cried out mockingly. 'So why don't you come out with your hands raised above your head and free that

236

young woman? And I give you my pledge, for old time's sake, not to shoot you down.'

'Sounds reasonable,' Billy shouted. 'But what's in it for you?'

Another weird and sinister laugh. 'What's in it for me is this. You come out and free the girl and you forget about me and ride back to Freshwater. Then we both get what we we want and live to fight another day. How would that be, Billy?'

That would be good except that Miss Nancy and me — one of us — gets killed, Billy calculated.

'Keep talking to Toms,' he said to Miss Emily. 'Can you do that to distract him while I make my break?'

'Yes, I can do that,' Miss Emily promised, in a voice as harsh as a determined man. 'Just as long as I get to kill him for what he did to Nancy.'

'Then I go,' Billy said.

Little Shoes had been quietly lining up the horses and they were quivering.

Billy had thought of riding out to the

rock but guessed that before he swung up into the saddle hot lead would start to fly. So he would plunge forward clinging to the side of a horse Indian fashion and lunge in a series of swerves and plunges towards the rock. It would take no longer than half a minute but it would be the longest half-minute of his life. He got a firm grip on the horse's mane and tried to forget the bullets and remember the feeling of invincibility he had felt in the valley when he started in pursuit of Toms. But it wasn't like that. He fixed his eye on Miss Nancy hanging from the rock and, when Little Shoes slapped the horses' rumps and yelled high Indian war cries, the horse he was clinging to reared and bolted straight up the pass towards the drooping girl, and Billy hung on, hoping for some kind of miracle to see him through.

Maybe he heard the crack of gunfire from above and the noise like thunder reverberating round the pass but he paid no heed. As the horse bucked and ran he saw the pitiful face of the girl who had waved the silk scarf at him and worn the subtle perfume, raised in hope to greet him. A look of wonder and astonishment and hope sprang on to her face as he plunged towards her. The horse bucked again and he lost his grip and fell and rolled.

Half winded, he crawled to the girl and slid his knife under the rope and sliced through it and she fell towards him. He tried to grab her and drag her to the sparse cover of a cactus when he felt the red-hot stab of a poker sear his left arm and knew he'd been hit. The bullet had been thrown from high on his right and had pierced his left arm from behind just below the shoulder. He fell spread-eagled across the girl as though trying to shield her. As they rolled together beside the cactus the two horses bolted on beyond the rock and up the gorge. Billy swung to look up at the ridge on his right and saw a man rising as if to get a bead on him again to finish him off. Hickory face again! Such a pity to die at the hands of a skunk like that! But, as Jeremiah Dandy rose to take his final shot, a kind of miracle occurred. Suddenly an arrow sprouted from his chest. He looked down in amazement, dropped his gun and clutched at the arrow, and then pitched forward over the rock and hung jerking and suspended like a pinned butterfly.

But guns were still booming away when Billy passed out.

* * *

When he came round again, he saw the face of Little Shoes like the vision of an angel bending towards him, and he thought he was on his way to the pearly gates. But he shook the vision off and tried to struggle to his feet. As he moved, the pain in his left shoulder sprang at him like the bite of a yellow-fanged grizzly.

'What happened?' he roared.

'Girl OK.' Little Shoes was smiling

grimly. 'One man up there dead.'

Billy squinted up through his pain and saw the body of Dandy draped over the rock with two arrows, one in its neck and one in its chest.

'You hit him!' he gasped.

'Me not hit,' Little Shoes said. 'Yellow Wolf hit plenty good.' These were Yellow Wolf's arrows, more accurate and more deadly than a handgun or a Winchester at that range especially in the hands of a skilled bowman. Yellow Wolf had brought the well rested horses quickly behind them up the pass and, when they paused and the voice of Toms ricocheted off the rocks, he had read the situation like the best of scouts and had swarmed up the cliff to their right to outflank Dandy whom he guessed was on the opposite bluff.

'What happened to Miss Nancy?' Billy croaked.

'Miss Nancy alive. Miss Emily give her treatment,' Little Shoes affirmed.

Miss Emily was cradling Nancy's head and holding a water bottle up to her mouth and she was drinking, not like a lady, but with real greedy thirst.

Billy rolled over and saw Yellow Wolf standing on the trail with a grin on his face that spelled pride.

'What happened to Toms?' Billy said.

'Toms go,' Little Shoes said. 'When Dandy die, he pull out fast after Yellow Wolf shoot across the pass at him.'

Billy staggered to his feet. He peered up at the ridge on the left and couldn't believe what had happened: Toms had pulled out and fled. Was that possible? But that was Toms's style. He knew how to calculate his chances and, when necessary, he would hightail it and live to spread his poison another day.

'Where are the horses?' Billy demanded. 'Bring me a horse!'

Though his shoulder ached like hell, he was standing now and the searing pain in his shoulder skewered his soul and made him as mad as a bull goaded by a matador.

'What you do?' Little Shoes said.

'I'm going after that bastard so he can't do more damage in this unhappy world,' Billy announced.

'Listen, you can't do that.' Miss Emily had turned from tending Miss Nancy and peered up in to his eyes. 'You're wounded; you're bleeding. Leave Toms and let him go. You need all your strength to get yourself back to Freshwater Creek.'

But Yellow Wolf was already leading up the fresh horses. 'I come too,' he said. 'Help you.'

Billy was already swinging up on to the back of what he considered to be the best and freshest horse. 'You stay back. This is between me and Toms. Take these ladies back down the pass. Maybe I'll come later.'

The two Indians nodded solemnly and before Miss Emily started pleading with him again, Billy touched the horse's side and moved on up the pass.

★   ★   ★

But this was no impulsive action. As he rode, Billy checked the Winchester he had taken from Miss Emily and the Colt revolver he had picked up from one of the dead men close by the cabin. He had counted the bullets in the gunbelt and guessed he had more than he needed. So he rode on knowing that Toms must be ahead of him. He had no other way to go.

Billy no longer felt like an eagle soaring above the mountains. He was simply a man with iron in his soul riding on knowing he must sooner or later catch up with a killer.

Yet his thoughts went back to the days when he was young, the days he had ridden with Toms. There was no denying it: Toms had been good to him in his own way. Billy had seen his charming side. Toms could talk. Somewhere early on he had received education and he knew how to deliver his thoughts in speech. It would have been easy now to turn back as Miss Emily had suggested. Even now as he rode on, taking his time, he could turn back and nothing would be lost. Yet the thought of Slam Beardsley, the gambling man who had helped him, who had cared for him when the bullet had creased his skull, made him determined.

So he rode on.

The pain in his shoulder had lessened. Or was it that he was losing touch with the world? His head was beginning to cloud and he felt like a goldfish swimming in a bowl of murky water. The path widened again into a more open area with green vegetation and a waterfall that fell in cold blue water into a gorge where no man could ride.

Billy shook his head clear. Close to the edge of the waterfall a solitary figure sat astride a horse. It was Toms and Toms seemed to be waiting fatalistically as Billy approached.

'So you couldn't stop yourself, could you?' Toms jeered. 'I declare you ain't got the sense you were born with. You had to come on and get yourself killed.'

'It's either me or you,' Billy said. 'There's no way back.'

Toms gave a slow nod and glanced about. 'Where are those Indian friends of yours?' he said. 'Did you arrange for them to creep up and kill me while we speak?'

Billy grinned. He felt almost calm. 'You think I'd do that, Toms?' he said. 'You think I learned those low down tricks from you?'

Toms put his head on one side. 'Well, you learned good enough to creep up to Big King by the back door instead of riding up and knocking good and clear on the front door now, didn't you? Or did you learn that from your Indian friends?'

Billy eased himself in the saddle. He knew Toms could talk for the rest of the day, if necessary, until he felt like a gopher mesmerized by a snake. He could see Toms's hand resting close to the gun on his hip. He knew from the past that Toms was quick. That Colt revolver could be out quicker than a snake bit and he would be dead.

'See you got yourself winged in the shoulder,' the older man said. 'It looks bad. You're still bleeding, man. Your life is draining away in blood. Another few minutes you're going to slide from that saddle and hit the dust.' Toms glanced to his left on to the trail. 'Come to mention it, Billy, this might be quite a good place to die. Did you think of that? Is that why you followed me so close? Find a good place to die?'

Billy knew it had to end soon. It was too late to go back now. Either he or Toms must die.

'I don't have any immediate plans about that,' he said. 'I come to take you in, that's all. Now I suggest you unbuckle your gunbelt and let your Colt revolver drop down over the side of that horse. Then we can ride back good and slow to Freshwater and wait for them to ship you up to Laramie like they were going to.'

Toms laughed. 'Think again,' he said.

'There's no way I'm going to Laramie. There's no way I was ever going to Laramie. I thought you knew that.'

'I did guess at that,' Billy said. 'Otherwise they'd have trussed you up like a chicken ready for the oven.'

'Well, I guess money and gold are a great thing, Billy. You should try and get yourself a stake.'

'Just so long as you unbuckle that gunbelt and let it drop, we can talk about that later.'

Toms looked him straight in the eye as an eagle might look at jack-rabbit. He was laughing when he said, 'OK, Billy, have it your way.'

His hands went to the buckle of his gunbelt but Billy was ready. When Toms made a play for his gun it was already a tenth of second too late. The Colt came up almost into line, but Billy had already drawn his weapon and he held it out straight The two spurts of flame came almost simultaneously.

Billy felt no pain as his horse reared and pranced.

Toms had a momentary look of surprise on his face as he cocked his gun for a second shot, but the second shot never came. He sat like a figure carved out of wood, then pitched over backwards into the dust.

25

Next day towards sundown, the towns-people of Freshwater were going about their business much the same as usual. The Reverend Jim Mullins had just emerged from his little shack that served as a church where he had been conducting a service in memory of Marshal Eldridge Leaver who lay wrapped in ice in the town mortuary. The marshal might have been buried by now only the powers-that-be needed to conduct a postmortem to determine how he had died and how it was that the criminal Toms had got away from custody so easily. Some blamed the marshal himself for treating the matter so casually. Others were inclined to blame Sheriff Watts for acting so ineffectually and not putting out a posse to hunt for the killer and his gang. And some threw the blame on Gus Felixstowe and the

Walker Company for their badly maintained stagecoaches. Rumours were flying everywhere and wild tales floated through the air like balloons on the Fourth of July.

They had also remembered the coach driver Old Jake in their prayers. Everyone had liked him and thought it was unjust and tragic that he had been flung off the coach like that and catapulted into the ravine below. Some comforted themselves with the thought that was just the way Old Jake would have wanted it, being hurled straight through the pearly gates like that.

There was also a good deal of speculation about Billy Bandro and the gambler Slam Beardsley. Some even said that Billy had fought off a band of thirty or so killers and run off to Mexico with Nancy Partridge. That was on account of his gallantry towards her when she embarked on the stage, and because of what Sheriff Watts had observed between them on the night before the coach left on its ill-fated journey to Laramie. Watts had never liked the younger and better-looking man, so he was only too pleased to encourage the poison of gossip to drip into people's ears.

At that very moment, as Jim Mullins stepped out from his church, the sheriff came swaggering towards him with his thumbs hooked into his gunbelt below his ample belly and with the stump of a dead cigar sticking from the corner of his mouth. 'Well now, Reverend, it's right good of you to put on that service for the departed. Eldridge Leaver was a good man though we didn't know much about him here in Freshwater.' He loosened his thumb from his gunbelt and raised his hand. 'Oh, I know we should have given Leaver better protection, but that's the way he wanted it. He thought it best to keep things quiet so he could get that criminal critter to Laramie without much fuss. I offered to provide them with outriders but poor Leaver was too proud and stiff necked to allow that deal.'

Jim Mullins treated Watts to one of his ironic grins, the sort most people saw and hid their faces from when he talked about the good life and the dangers of hellfire on a Sunday. 'Well now, Mr Watts,' he drawled, 'It seems Marshal Leaver gave his life trying to uphold the law. So we must praise him and thank the Lord for that and hope he's been taken up to a better place.'

'True, true,' intoned the sheriff, hat in hand. 'By the by, I did hear Miss Lou Lou had been struck low with some sickness or other. Do you happen to know how that poor girl is faring?'

Mullins shot him another ironic glance. 'I hear she's got the flu or some such. Hasn't been able to perform in the saloon for two nights. Maybe it's a sign from Heaven. Mrs Mullins went to visit with her. I believe she took her a bowl of her own homemade broth and very good it is too. The woman hasn't much appetite, but I think she might recover in good time, thank the Lord.'

'Thank the Lord indeed,' Sheriff Watts

intoned. Though he never stepped into the little church himself he could switch to a pious air as quickly as strapping on his gunbelt.

The sun was close to kissing the distant hills and the light was getting dim as the two men turned to look along Main Street — the only street of any importance in Freshwater Creek — to witness a slight disturbance in the form of a slow advancing cavalcade of riders. Mullins had sharp eyes, especially for the woes and mischiefs of mankind. Some said if he hadn't been a preacher he could have been an ace reporter on the The Freshwater Star, or some such newspaper.

What he saw in the early evening light surprised him: a man with his left arm held close in a sling; two very bedraggled women as pale and drawn as Halloween witches; and two Indians riding proud as wooden hickory poles. Between the women and the Indians came two horses with bodies thrown across their backs.

As they approached, someone spread the news and soon men and women and children came swarming out of cabins and stores to marvel and stand with wondering eyes to stare at them, among them Gus Felixstowe who gawped like a stranded catfish at the leading rider.

'Why, that's Billy Bandro, I do declare!' said the Reverend Mullins.

Watts shaded his eyes and squinted out at the approaching riders. 'I do believe you're right!' he said somewhat less enthusiastically. In the fading light nobody would have noticed the change in his high crimson complexion to something between yellow and cactus green.

The cavalcade drew to a halt in front of the Bronco Saloon. The piano had stopped tinkling and even the card players had taken a break. Stan Bird's Eye ran out to the veranda in his newfangled bowler hat. He was grinning, like a chimpanzee at a tea party. And Johnny Steegles came out too, wiping his hands on his green apron.

When they saw the state of the bedraggled band, they stopped clapping and gazed in wonder. Johnny Steegles hurried down the step to give Billy a hand to help him off his horse, but Billy held up his arm and dismounted on his own.

'You got any of that good swill you dish out?' he said, 'because I could drink up an ocean of that booze.'

That lightened the tone considerably.

Little Shoes and Yellow Wolf had already dismounted and were helping Miss Nancy and Miss Emily down from their horses.

'Don't fuss so,' Miss Emily said, waving her hand, and that gave rise to more laughter.

Now people were crowding round the two bodies.

'That there is the outlaw Toms,' someone shouted.

'And this one's the gambling man Slam Beardsley,' another man hooted. 'He never did pay me that ten dollars he owed me.'

'You'll get your rotten money,' Billy growled. 'Get Slam into the mortuary and lay him out with due respect. That man was as brave as Hercules!'

'What about this one?' someone asked with his hand on Toms's body. 'What do we do with him?'

Billy shrugged. 'Better ask Sheriff Watts,' he said. 'They'll probably send someone to identify the body and make sure he's dead.'

There was a hoot of laughter and a cheer.

'Whoever killed Toms there could be a reward,' Jim Mullins said.

Somebody said, 'Could be a million dollars!'

Everyone laughed and cheered. Sheriff Watts turned from green to puce but in the excitement nobody noticed.

Watts still had the stub of his dead cigar in the corner of his mouth as he approached Billy. 'So you got Toms after all?' he said.

'We got Toms and a few more up there by Big King, thanks to these two brave Crow men.'

Little Shoes and Yellow Wolf stood stone-faced and bewildered before the sheriff. Watts hadn't talked much with Indians, but he nodded. 'Then we owe you a lot,' he said, between his nicotine-stained teeth.

'Ain't you going to arrest me?' Billy said.

Watts shifted his cigar from one side of his mouth to the other. 'We'll talk about that later.'

'I don't know what all the fuss is about,' Miss Emily crowed. 'We only did what we had to do. Come on, Nancy, we must get ourselves up to the hotel and get ourselves a hot bath and some good nourishing food.'

Men and women were crowding around the two women and the reporter and owner of The Freshwater Star was already trying to get their story for his paper. But Miss Nancy turned back and, though she was bedraggled as if she had been pulled between cactus plants and bruising rocks, she still looked surprisingly pretty.

'Billy,' she said with a look of tenderness in her eyes. She laid her hand on his arm. He remembered the faded perfume and the silk kerchief and the soft feminine words. 'Slam Beardsley was a hero, but you were more than a hero. You were a very brave man up there and I must thank you for my life.'

She leaned forward, raised her head, and kissed him full on the mouth. Billy had seldom been kissed like that before and he stood aghast for nearly ten seconds as she turned again and headed for the Grand Hotel.

Then he shook his head. 'Where's Lou Lou?' he asked. 'I don't see Lou Lou.'

'Lou Lou's here.' He heard the familiar voice, the voice he had heard so often before in the Bronco Saloon and now he saw her not with the painted face of a dancing girl but with the pale face of a woman who had suffered.

'You're sick,' he said. 'How come? You mustn't be sick. I've been counting on you to be well.'

She reached out to touch him on the arm. 'I didn't think you were coming back, Billy,' she said. 'But you are back. What happened to your arm?'

Billy held his head on one side and grinned. 'I guess I stood in the way of a stray bullet. Now wasn't that a dumb thing to do?'

'We must take care to get you better,' she said.

★   ★   ★

In the upstairs room in the Bronco Saloon after Billy had taken a bath, he sat down to eat. He knew he was hungry but he didn't realize how hungry he was until the food was placed before him on the table.

As he was about to take his first mouthful, Lou Lou crept into the room like a shadow. She sat down opposite him.

'You should be resting in your bed,' she declared. 'You look terrible pale. I thought you'd never come back.'

Billy grinned. 'There was a moment I thought I'd be food for coyotes. But I came back a little broken at the edges, and you're here too. That's the big deal.'

Billy didn't know how to speak of what was in his heart. He had never had enough practice or confidence.

Lou Lou was staring at him earnestly and wide-eyed across the table. She looked a deal better already, he noticed. 'What happens now?' she asked him, with scarcely a breath.

Billy paused in his eating. He put down his fork and stared right back at her and saw her immediately as a different woman. All the make-up had gone and he saw again the real woman behind the mask, and he liked what he saw.

'What happens now?' he repeated.

Lou Lou took in a deep breath like a woman who is about to swim for a hundred feet underwater. 'Are you going to marry that woman, Billy?' she asked.

'Which woman?' he said.

'Don't fool with me, Billy. You know the woman I mean.'

Billy looked down at his steak reflectively and considered a moment. 'Well, you know what,' he said, 'I don't think I will marry that woman you mention. One thing, I haven't asked her yet and she hasn't asked me.' He grinned again and his eyes switched to Lou Lou's pale hand resting on the white tablecloth.

'I think she wants you to,' she said quietly. 'I saw it in her eyes.'

He raised his eyes to look at her again. His grin turned to a smile. 'You did, did you?'

'I did,' she declared.

Billy shook his head slowly. 'A close brush with the big D makes a man think, you know. Like you said that night here in the saloon, a man needs a change of occupation if he isn't going to become a bum or a piece of wandering tumbleweed. So maybe I should turn my hand and become a writer after all.'

'You could do that, Billy,' she agreed with enthusiasm. 'You really could.'

'So, as soon as these tired ribs have rested up and my busted shoulder heals, I think . . . I think I may light out and go to California.'

'To California!' Her eyes opened wide and then dimmed again. 'That will be nice for you, Billy.'

'Yes, that will be real nice.' He reached and took her pale hand between his rough fingers. 'It will be real nice . . . ' He looked up directly into her eyes and stayed. 'But I don't aim to go alone.'

'You don't?' Her eyes looked deep into his.

'No,' he murmured, 'I don't. I won't go alone. I'm taking you with me, if you'll come.'

She was smiling suddenly.

'Will you come with me, Lou Lou?' he asked.

She held her breath for half a second. 'Is that a real proposal, Billy?'

'That's a real gold-plated proposal,

Lou Lou. I can't get down on my knee right now, but that's a genuine proposal.'

There was another pause, slightly longer this time.

'Then you know, Billy, I think I'm going to accept,' she said.

Somewhere down below Stan Bird's Eye struck a chord on the piano and it seemed to reverberate through the whole of the Bronco Saloon and right into the town of Freshwater Creek itself! And even beyond!

THE END

We do hope that you have enjoyed reading this large print book.

Did you know that all of our titles are available for purchase?

We publish a wide range of high quality large print books including:
Romances, Mysteries, Classics
General Fiction
Non Fiction and Westerns

Special interest titles available in large print are:
The Little Oxford Dictionary
Music Book, Song Book
Hymn Book, Service Book

Also available from us courtesy of Oxford University Press:
Young Readers' Dictionary
(large print edition)
Young Readers' Thesaurus
(large print edition)

For further information or a free brochure, please contact us at:
Ulverscroft Large Print Books Ltd.,
The Green, Bradgate Road, Anstey,
Leicester, LE7 7FU, England.
Tel: (00 44) 0116 236 4325
Fax: (00 44) 0116 234 0205

379072

Other titles in the
Linford Western Library:

SILVER GALORE

John Dyson

The mysterious southern belle, Careen Langridge, has come West to escape death threats from fanatical Confederates. Is she still being pursued? Should she marry Captain Robbie Randall? The Mexican Artiside Luna has his own plans . . . With gambler and fast-gun Luke Short he murders Randall's men and targets Careen. Can the amiable cowboy Tex Anderson and his pal, Pancho, impose rough justice as with guns blazing they go to Careen's aid?